HEAD OVER HEELS

Lila laughed. "If I win, you write my term paper. And if *you* win, I write yours. How does that sound?"

Jessica swallowed. If she lost the bet, she'd have *two* term papers to write. And at this point she could barely imagine writing one!

But she wasn't about to let Lila see how worried she was. "You're on," Jessica said cheerfully.

"Fine," said Lila. "We'll make the carnival the cutoff point. Just think, if Bruce and Regina break up before then, you won't have to worry about your term paper!"

And if they don't, Jessica thought uneasily, *I might as well hang myself.* She looked across the cafeteria to where Bruce and Regina were sitting and shook her head. *This bet is too important to lose,* Jessica thought. *If Bruce and Regina don't break up on their own in a few days, I'm going to have to do my best to help them!*

Bantam Books in the Sweet Valley High Series
Ask your bookseller for the books you have missed

SWEET VALLEY HIGH

HEAD OVER HEELS

Written by
Kate William

Created by
FRANCINE PASCAL

BANTAM BOOKS
TORONTO · NEW YORK · LONDON · SYDNEY · AUCKLAND

RL 6, IL age 12 and up

HEAD OVER HEELS

A Bantam Book / December 1986
9 printings through February 1988

ISBN 0-553-27444-9

Published simultaneously in the United States and Canada

Bantam Books are published by Bantam Books, a division of Bantam Doubleday
Dell Publishing Group, Inc. Its trademark, consisting of the words "Bantam
Books" and the portrayal of a rooster, is Registered in U.S. Patent and Trademark
Office and in other countries. Marca Registrada. Bantam Books, 666 Fifth Avenue,
New York, New York 10103.

PRINTED IN THE UNITED STATES OF AMERICA

O   18 17 16 15 14 13 12 11 10 9

HEAD OVER HEELS

One

"Jessica Wakefield," Elizabeth called, knocking firmly on the door of her twin sister's bedroom, "were you planning on waking up at some point this morning?"

Hearing her twin's groan, Elizabeth pushed open the door to Jessica's bedroom. "Come on, Jess," she urged, pulling up the blinds and letting light pour into the room. "Good Lord," she said, looking around her. "It looks like you've been dynamiting in here. How can you sleep in this mess?"

Jessica sat up in the rumpled sheets, stretching her slim arms over her tousled blond hair and yawning. "What time is it, Liz?" she asked crossly. "It feels like it's about four in the morning."

1

Elizabeth laughed. It was like Jessica not to have a clock in her room. She lived by what her parents sometimes referred to as Jessica Standard Time. Being on time was *not* one of her concerns.

Apart from a mole on Elizabeth's right shoulder, the twins were identical down to the tiny dimple in each left cheek. They were both sixteen years old, though Elizabeth was born four minutes before Jessica. Both had shoulder-length, sun-streaked blond hair, sparkling blue-green eyes, and model-slim, five-foot-six-inch figures. Even the gold lavalieres dangling around their necks were identical—presents from their parents on their sixteenth birthday.

But the resemblance between the twins was only skin deep. Elizabeth, who wrote the "Eyes and Ears" gossip column for *The Oracle*, the student newspaper at Sweet Valley High, wanted to be a serious writer one day. That was why, as she often explained to Todd Wilkins, her steady boyfriend, she tried her hardest to be objective. Organized, good-natured, and fair as possible— that was how Elizabeth's friends described her. Jessica, on the other hand, never planned more than one day at a time, though she threw herself into every project—and every new relationship—with astounding energy.

"It's eight o'clock," Elizabeth told her twin

firmly. "And it'll probably take you half an hour to find your closet in this mess!"

"It's cozy in here, Liz," Jessica said defensively, leaping out of bed and heading straight for the mirror over her dresser.

Elizabeth laughed. Jessica's room had always been a sore point in the Wakefield household. The rest of the attractive, split-level home was nicely decorated and tidy as a pin. But Jessica's room—which was sometimes referred to as "The Hershey Bar" because she had insisted on painting her walls chocolate brown—was always a mess. She rarely bothered to pick her clothes up from the floor.

"It feels like another world in here," Jessica told her twin proudly.

"It sure does," Elizabeth said, shaking her head as she stepped over an enormous pile of clothing on her way to the door. "Try to hurry, Jess," she called from the hallway. "I'm supposed to meet Todd before homeroom this morning."

Downstairs, in the sun-filled, Spanish-style kitchen, Alice Wakefield was mixing orange juice in a glass pitcher. "Morning, Mom," Elizabeth said, giving her mother an affectionate hug. "You look pretty today," she added, glancing admiringly at her mother's flowered dress.

"A client's coming over to look at some floor plans," her mother said, smiling.

Alice Wakefield worked as an interior designer. With her blond hair, bright-blue eyes, and trim figure, it was easy to see where the twins had gotten their good looks. People often mistook Alice Wakefield for the twins' older sister.

"Looks like another beautiful day," Ned Wakefield exclaimed, hurrying into the kitchen and dropping an affectionate kiss on his wife's cheek. "Where's your better half?" he teased Elizabeth, pouring himself a cup of coffee.

Elizabeth giggled. "Probably bulldozing a path to her closet," she told him.

The corners of Mr. Wakefield's eyes crinkled with laughter. Broad-shouldered and dark-haired, with warm, dark eyes, he looked to Elizabeth like an older version of her brother Steven, who was finishing his first year of college.

"Give her a hug for me, will you?" Mr. Wakefield said. "If I don't hurry I'm going to miss my meeting this morning." Ned Wakefield was a successful lawyer whose office was located in downtown Sweet Valley.

"At this rate, she probably won't be downstairs before you come home for dinner!" Elizabeth laughed as she poured herself a bowl of cereal.

Taking a last gulp of coffee and waving at Elizabeth and her mother, Mr. Wakefield hurried outside to the garage.

"Mom, do you mind if I take the Fiat this morning? Mr. Collins has called a meeting of the carnival committee after school today."

"The carnival committee?" Alice Wakefield looked blank for a minute.

"To raise money for handicapped children," Elizabeth reminded her. "It's not a real carnival," she added. "A group of us at school is putting it together, and I'm the chairperson. It'll just be a tent or two with games and refreshments. But Mr. Collins thinks we can raise a fair amount of money, especially now that we're getting sponsors from the community."

"Now I remember," her mother said. "When is it supposed to take place?"

"A week from Saturday." Elizabeth sighed. "That's only twelve days, and we've still got so much to do!"

"Well, you're welcome to the car," Mrs. Wakefield said. "I don't need it today. Just drive safely."

"Drive safely where?" Jessica asked, strolling into the kitchen and taking an orange from the basket on the table.

"School," Elizabeth said wryly. "Or have you forgotten?"

"I wish I *could* forget," Jessica said, flinging herself down on a chair. "That stupid term paper is giving me nightmares."

5

"Try working on it during daylight hours," Elizabeth said and smiled.

"Fifteen pages!" Jessica moaned. "How am I supposed to fit that in on top of everything else?"

"History teachers should be better organized," Elizabeth agreed. "They really should schedule homework assignments around dates and cheerleading practice."

"OK, girls," Alice Wakefield said, bringing a carton of milk to the table. "I'm going to go put my makeup on. Careful with the car, you two, and I'll see you both tonight."

"Jess, do you have any good ideas for the carnival?" Elizabeth asked, turning the red Fiat down the shady street.

Jessica shot a quick look at her twin, who was concentrating on the road in front of her. "I don't suppose you'd trade me a few pointers on my history paper for some carnival ideas?" she asked craftily.

Elizabeth checked the traffic in the rearview mirror. "You're right," she said firmly. "I wouldn't. Come on, Jess. We've got less than two weeks to get this thing organized, and we really need some help. Besides," she added, "it's such a good cause. The money we raise will be donated to a special fund at Fowler Memorial Hospital to help handicapped children."

"I'll think about it," Jessica said absently, her eyes on the lush green panorama of the roadside near Sweet Valley High. "Hey," she said suddenly, leaning forward, "isn't that Regina Morrow in Bruce Patman's car?"

Elizabeth gave her twin a quick look. "It is," she confirmed, maneuvering the Fiat into the lane next to Bruce's shiny black Porsche. "They've been seeing an awful lot of each other lately, haven't they?" Elizabeth asked, glancing at Jessica to view her reaction.

Bruce Patman was the only son of Henry and Marie Patman, one of the richest and most powerful couples in Sweet Valley. Bruce was a senior at Sweet Valley High. Dark-haired, handsome, and powerfully built, he had a reputation as a lady's man and a snob. Even his license plate number—1BRUCE1—displayed his arrogance. Elizabeth didn't like Bruce Patman one bit. He had tried to take advantage of her after her motorcycle accident when she was suffering from memory loss and wasn't herself. And she knew Jessica didn't think much of him either. At one point Jessica had fallen head over heels in love with him. Elizabeth had never seen her sister so affected by a boyfriend. The fact that things had ended badly—and that Bruce's behavior had caused the breakup—explained the stormy expression on her twin's face as they overtook the black Porsche.

"I can't understand why Regina would get mixed up with a jerk like Bruce Patman," Jessica said sullenly, pulling her blond hair back from her face.

Elizabeth was too tactful to point out that Jessica herself had once found Bruce the most fascinating male in the world. "I know," she agreed. "I have to admit I don't think much of the idea. Regina is so incredibly nice," she added, pulling into the parking lot next to Sweet Valley High.

Bruce pulled his Porsche up beside them and was leaping out to open the door for Regina.

"Good Lord," Jessica muttered. "I wonder what he's up to with the Prince Charming act."

"That's the strange thing," Elizabeth said in a low voice. "I've never seen Bruce act this way before. He seems to be killing Regina with kindness. He even meets her after every class so he can have a few minutes with her."

"I'm sure it won't last," Jessica snapped, grabbing her books and jumping out of the car. "Thanks for the ride, Liz. I'm going to find Cara before homeroom."

Elizabeth shook her head as she watched her twin bound across the parking lot. Jessica didn't seem crazy about the idea of Bruce and Regina as a couple, she thought.

It was funny, Elizabeth mused, gathering her books and getting out of the car. As far as looks went, Bruce and Regina seemed like a perfect couple. But then, Regina looked perfect no matter who she was standing next to.

With her long, black hair, high cheekbones, and perfect ivory complexion, Regina Morrow was a natural beauty. The Morrows had moved to Sweet Valley just that year, and Regina's spectacular looks had caused a great deal of attention. She had even been approached by a local modeling agency, which had arranged to have her picture on the cover of a recent issue of *Ingenue* magazine.

But beauty wasn't all that made Regina Morrow special, Elizabeth thought, catching sight of Todd across the parking lot and quickening her steps to meet him. Regina had been almost completely deaf since birth. Years of training in a school in Connecticut had taught her to read lips so well that some people couldn't tell she couldn't hear them. And because Regina could distinguish tones, her voice hadn't been affected by her handicap.

The real difference, Elizabeth thought, was that Regina didn't take anything for granted as so many people did. She loved being alive and it showed in everything she did. No wonder people liked her so much and were so much happier when she was around!

"Hey, where've you been?" Todd asked, giving Elizabeth a warm hug and kissing the tip of her nose. "I've been looking all over for you. Mr. Collins wants to know how we're doing with the carnival plans."

"Sorry I'm so late," Elizabeth told him, smiling up into his coffee-brown eyes. "Jessica was in slow motion this morning. Or at least she was until she saw Bruce and Regina together. *That* speeded her up."

"I can imagine." Todd grinned and slipped his arm around her. "Hey, maybe we can get them to do a booth at the carnival," he added, laughing. "We'll call it 'Beauty and the Beast.' "

Elizabeth laughed, but she felt uneasy as she and Todd walked into the cool interior of Sweet Valley High. She wasn't sure why, but she had felt strangely protective of Regina ever since the girl had moved to Sweet Valley. As far as Elizabeth knew, Regina didn't have much experience with boys. She had lived a sheltered life, and Elizabeth felt that Bruce Patman wasn't the safest bet for a first boyfriend.

"I hope she doesn't get hurt," Elizabeth told Todd, giving his hand a warm squeeze. "You have to remember," she added softly, slipping her arm around him, "not all guys are as wonderful as you are."

"I never forget it for a second," Todd joked, kissing the top of Elizabeth's head. "You're right, though," he added more seriously. "I'm a little worried, myself. Regina's such a nice girl, and I don't trust Bruce Patman."

"Well," Elizabeth said, opening the door to her locker and putting her books inside, "I guess we'll just have to watch what happens."

"And hope the Beast doesn't break the Beauty's heart," Todd added, a concerned expression on his face.

Two

"Don't you think the carnival committee deserves better food?" Winston Egbert joked, spearing a hot dog with his fork and raising it in the air.

Enid Rollins laughed. "We should've picked a better place to meet, Liz," she told Elizabeth, who was furiously jotting notes on a pad next to her lunch tray.

Elizabeth looked up at her best friend and grinned. "What better place for brainstorming than the eye of the hurricane?" she pointed out. Elizabeth and Todd were sitting across from Enid and Winston in the middle of the crowded Sweet Valley High cafeteria, trying to organize themselves before the meeting with Mr. Collins after

12

school. But Winston, a tall, lanky boy generally known as the class clown, was contributing more merriment than constructive advice. He had just discovered that by pounding an empty milk carton with his fist he could fire the last drops of milk at the person next to him.

"Quit it, Egbert," Todd said cheerfully, leaning across the table to see what Elizabeth had written. "Hey, when is Mr. Collins going to announce who the parent adviser is? I think we need some fresh ideas."

"After school today, I think," Elizabeth told him, putting the cap back on her pen and looking at the preliminary list she'd drawn up. "I hope so, anyway." she said. "At the rate we're going, we'll never get this carnival together!"

"Liz! Todd! We've been looking for you everywhere," a voice called. Elizabeth turned to see Olivia Davidson and her boyfriend, Roger Barrett Patman, approaching with their trays.

"How's it going?" Olivia asked, glancing at Elizabeth's notebook as she set the tray down. Olivia was the arts editor for *The Oracle*, and she and Elizabeth had often collaborated on projects for the newspaper.

"I'm the only one who has an idea for a booth so far," Winston told her. "I'm going to let people throw pies at me for a dollar a shot."

Everyone laughed. Olivia pushed her frizzy brown hair back from her face and looked down at her lunch with a grimace. "I don't think creativity and Sweet Valley High lunches mix." Roger reached across the table and gave her hand a gentle squeeze.

Olivia had loved Roger even before his identity as Bruce Patman's cousin was discovered. Before Roger had learned he was really the illegitimate son of Bruce's uncle—dead now for many years—Roger had been the poorest boy in the class. Now he lived in the Patmans' enormous estate on the hill overlooking Sweet Valley. Elizabeth had wondered at first how Roger would react to being part of a millionaire's family, but by now it was apparent that Roger was as down to earth as he'd always been. And he and Olivia were as fond of each other as ever.

"Boy, that cousin of mine has really gone off the deep end this time!" Roger exclaimed, watching Bruce pull a chair out for Regina on the other side of the cafeteria.

"What do you mean?" Todd asked curiously, catching Elizabeth's eye.

Roger shook his head. "I don't know," he said slowly, opening his carton of milk and taking a big gulp. "But I'd say this time he really has fallen hard!"

Olivia leaned forward, her hazel eyes dancing. "It's incredible," she confided. "Bruce is like a completely new person! He actually asked me how I've been when he answered the phone last

14

night. And"—she shook her head and giggled—"more to the point, he listened when I told him!"

"Revolutionary," Todd said, grinning.

"I've never seen him so friendly," Roger went on. "I think he's flipped over Regina."

"So you *really* think Bruce is serious about her?" Elizabeth asked.

"I'll tell you what *I* think," Winston interrupted, punching Roger's empty milk carton so the spray hit Todd on the arm. "*I* think we need to get back to the carnival."

"I guess you're right," Elizabeth said, pushing her lunch tray aside and picking up her note pad.

"Pretty romantic, don't you think?" Lila Fowler asked, waving the ice cream bar she was eating in the direction of Bruce and Regina, who were sitting across the cafeteria. There was a smirk on her pretty face.

Jessica followed Lila's gaze and shrugged. "You know Bruce," she said airily, pretending to concentrate on her lunch. "I bet it lasts about a week."

"Hmmmm," Lila said, her brown eyes narrowing as she watched Bruce kiss Regina on the cheek. "I can't imagine anyone staying interested in Regina for even that long," she said, flicking her wavy, light-brown hair behind one shoulder.

Jessica laughed. She knew there was no love lost between Lila and Regina. Lila Fowler had been the richest girl in school until Regina moved in. That in itself would have been enough to irritate Lila, who had always made a point of having the biggest or newest or best of everything. But Regina's beauty—and all the attention she got after her picture appeared on the cover of *Ingenue*—was more than Lila could bear. In fact, Lila had tried to convince The Lane Townsend Agency to put *her* on the cover instead of Regina. Lila was an attractive girl, but she wasn't model material. Or at least that was what the owner of the agency had told her. And hearing how perfect Regina was for the camera was all Lila had needed to decide that Regina Morrow was the most detestable girl at school.

"Just look at her," Lila seethed, pushing her food away in disgust. "She looks ridiculous in that purple dress. You'd think she was color blind, not deaf, the way she dresses."

Jessica turned to look across the cafeteria. "That dress isn't so bad. Bruce is the one who looks ridiculous. The way he stares at Regina you'd think he'd never seen a girl before."

"What I can't understand," Lila went on, "is how anyone could stand to be with her for more than five minutes. Regina Morrow is totally boring."

"Mmmm," Jessica muttered, opening her

notebook and scowling at its contents. She'd spent an entire period in the library, and she still wasn't any closer to finding a topic for her term paper.

"Jessica Wakefield, you're not even listening to me!" Lila cried, her mouth turning downward in a pout.

"Sorry," Jessica said, slamming her notebook shut. "I'm just worried about this stupid term paper. It counts for a third of our final grade, and I still don't have a topic."

Lila shrugged, licking the last bit of ice cream off its wooden stick. "Neither do I," she said without interest. "I can't imagine anything duller than history."

"Me either." She turned to take another look at Bruce and Regina.

"Cara told me Bruce has gone completely crazy over her," Lila confided, watching Jessica carefully to gauge her reaction. "He takes her absolutely everywhere. Cara says he can't stand to be away from her for even a *minute*."

Jessica flinched. Lila knew that one of the sorest points between Jessica and Bruce had been that he'd tried to get out of spending time with her by inventing phony excuses.

"Don't believe a word of it," Jessica said archly. "He's probably sneaking off to see those college girls of his while Regina's home studying."

Lila spread her hands out in front of her, admiring her manicure. "I don't know about that," she said, turning in their direction with a knowing smile. "Regina's even been invited up to the Patmans' house for dinner, Cara told me."

"I can't imagine anything worse," Jessica said furiously. The truth was that Jessica had always wanted to be accepted by the Patmans. She thought their house was beautiful, and she'd always pictured herself covered with jewelry, sweeping across the vast lawns of their estate. Having struck out with Bruce, she had made a play for Roger after his identity was disclosed. And it would have worked, she thought, if Roger hadn't been such a jerk about Olivia. Jessica had done her best to save Roger from social disaster, but in the end he had refused to be rescued. He'd stuck it out with Olivia, who dressed like a freak in Indian cotton dresses and funny sandals and didn't care about anything but drawing and poetry. A fate, Jessica thought, worse than death.

All in all, the Patmans were not Jessica's favorite subject these days. In her estimation, they fell even lower than history term papers, and she wished Lila would drop the topic.

"Well, dinner is one thing," Lila continued mercilessly, "but the most amazing news is that he bought her a ruby pendant. Cara saw it, and she said it's beautiful."

Jessica raised her eyebrows and said nothing, and Lila leaned forward, dropping her voice sympathetically. "Bruce never bought *you* anything expensive like that, did he?"

"No," Jessica said firmly, "he didn't. But I'll tell you something, Lila. Bruce Patman will never be serious about anyone besides himself. He'll get sick of Regina. I guarantee it. And he's so cheap, he's probably charging her rent for the necklace," she said, giggling.

Lila looked doubtful. "I don't know, Jess. I think you may be wrong."

"Trust me, Lila," Jessica said. "I give it two weeks. Tops."

Lila looked at Jessica with sudden interest. "Two weeks," she mused. "That would be about the time of the carnival, right?"

"That's right," Jessica said. "By the day of the carnival, they probably won't even be on speaking terms."

Lila gave Jessica a long look. "You sound pretty sure of yourself," she said at last. "I don't suppose you'd care to make a bet?"

Jessica thought fast. Lila's allowance was easily ten times as much as hers. She did some rapid calculation. How much did she owe Elizabeth? Not too much, she thought. Besides, she didn't want Lila to think she was backing out at this stage.

"Sure," Jessica said nonchalantly. "How much should we bet?"

Lila considered for a minute. "Let's not bet money," she suggested. "My father says it's vulgar."

Jessica looked confused. "What do we bet if we don't bet money?" she asked.

Lila's face lit up. "I've got a great idea!" she exclaimed. "We can bet term papers!"

Jessica stared at her. "Term papers? What do you mean?"

Lila laughed. "If I win, you write my term paper. And if *you* win, I write yours. How does that sound?"

Jessica swallowed. This was a lot worse than betting money. If she lost the bet, she'd have *two* term papers to write. And at this point she could barely imagine writing one!

Moreover, Jessica wasn't one bit sure that Bruce and Regina would break up. For all she knew, Bruce really *had* changed. It wasn't something she'd like to bet anything important on.

But Jessica wasn't about to let Lila see how worried she was. "You're on," she said cheerfully, reaching out to shake Lila's hand. "We'll bet our term papers."

If Lila was surprised that Jessica had accepted, she didn't show it. "Fine," she said. "We'll make the carnival the cutoff point. Just think, Jess," she added. "If Bruce and Regina break up before

20

then, you won't have to worry about your term paper!''

And if they don't, Jessica thought uneasily, *I might as well hang myself.* She looked across the cafeteria to where Bruce and Regina were sitting, and shook her head. *This bet is too important to lose*, Jessica thought. *If Bruce and Regina don't break up on their own in a few days, I'm going to have to do my best to help them.*

Three

Lila parked her lime-green Triumph in front of her father's office and across from the new building he was having built in downtown Sweet Valley. "I hope Daddy doesn't take too long," she murmured, checking her reflection in the rearview mirror. It was a gorgeous afternoon, and Lila wanted to go to the beach with Jessica and Cara. But the message she'd received from the office after lunch had been explicit. "Your father phoned this morning," the principal's secretary had told her. "He wants you to meet him at his office at four to discuss something."

Lila glanced impatiently at her watch. It was three forty-five, and she had a sneaking suspicion her father would keep her waiting. She had at least fifteen minutes to kill and nothing to do in the meantime. And the last place Lila could imagine finding anything interesting to watch was at the site of the half-completed Fowler building. In fact, the only thing that interested Lila about the Fowler business was the hefty allowance it provided her each month.

I wonder what Daddy wants to discuss, she thought, getting out of her car and leaning against the fence enclosing the site where the construction workers were moving piles of lumber. *I hope he's not cutting my allowance.*

While she was thinking about the meeting with her father, Lila watched the construction workers struggling with sacks of concrete. Her gaze kept returning to one young man in particular. He looked different from the others. For one thing, he was much younger—not more than eighteen or nineteen, Lila guessed. And he was handsome. His honey-brown, sun-lightened hair peeked out from under his work hat, and the muscles in his strong arms rippled as he lifted the heavy bags.

Seeing her watching him, the young man looked up at Lila and smiled. It was a cool, self-confident smile.

Lila smiled back at him, slightly surprised at herself. She didn't even usually *look* at construction workers, let alone encourage them. *I must be slipping*, she thought.

The young man sauntered casually over to the fence where Lila was standing. "Hi," he said, looking her up and down with the same cool, slow smile. "My name's Jack."

"Hello," Lila said casually. She felt slightly put out by his forward manner, but she couldn't help noticing how nice his eyes were. "My name is Lila." Then, adopting her most imperious tone, she added, "Lila *Fowler*."

"Aha," he said, smiling and looking at her more closely. "Fowler, like the building?" he asked, pointing behind him to the shell of what would eventually be the world headquarters for her father's computer company.

"Of course," Lila said archly. "That's my father."

Lila expected him to be impressed, but to her surprise he didn't seem to be. If anything, he just looked slightly amused. He tipped his head back a little, shading his eyes with one tanned hand, and squinted up at the sun.

"Nice day, don't you think?" he asked her.

"It's always nice here!" Lila giggled. "Aren't you from Sweet Valley?" she demanded.

"No," Jack told her, shaking his head.

Just then a whistle blew, signaling the end of the shift, and Jack grinned. "Oh, well. I'm afraid that whistle blows for me, to ruin an old quotation. But it's nice to have met you, Lila."

"Nice to have met you, too!" Lila called after him, watching him saunter back to join the others. What a strange young man, she thought, shaking her head a little as she left the fence. He didn't seem to fit her image of the average construction worker. For one thing, she had assumed that the minute he found out who she was, he'd change his manner. But he'd acted as if he and Lila were equals.

I wouldn't mind running into him again, Lila admitted to herself as she crossed the street to her father's office building. Something about him had aroused her curiosity. And Lila intended to find out more about him.

Mr. Collins was Elizabeth's favorite teacher at Sweet Valley High. And she wasn't the only one who felt that way. Everyone thought Mr. Collins looked like Robert Redford—strawberry blond hair, blue eyes. And he was still young enough to engage the interest of many of his students. Because Mr. Collins was the faculty adviser for *The Oracle*, Elizabeth had gotten to know him well. She often turned to him when she was worried about something or needed advice.

"Okay, carnival committee," Mr. Collins said now, sitting on the edge of his desk and facing the group before him. Elizabeth glanced around her to see who had shown up. Todd, of course, and Enid; Roger and Olivia; and Winston Egbert and Ken Matthews, the tall, good-looking captain of the football team. "Now, the first thing on the agenda is—"

Just then the door to Mr. Collins's room opened, and Regina Morrow walked in. "Come on in, Regina," Mr. Collins said cheerfully. "We're just getting started."

"Thanks, Mr. Collins," Regina said, slipping into an empty chair.

"As I was saying," Mr. Collins went on, the first thing we need to do is to draw up a list of booths we want, and put people in charge of them. The Sweet Valley PTA has chosen Skye Morrow, Regina's mother, to be our parent adviser," he added, looking at Regina and smiling. "Liz, as soon as you can arrange it, I'd like you to meet with Mrs. Morrow, and you two can put your ideas together. And now, I think I'll let you take over."

Elizabeth walked to the front of the room, taking her notebook with her. She flashed Todd a smile across the room. Elizabeth was delighted to be in charge of the carnival. She had a flair for organization, and this was a cause she believed in. "OK," she said, opening her notebook and picking up her pen. "Olivia, how would you like to be in charge of getting prizes and making decorations?" she asked. Aside from her role as arts editor, Olivia loved to paint and sew, and Elizabeth knew she would do a wonderful job of making the carnival festive.

"I'd love to," Olivia responded.

"By the way, Mr. Fowler has generously

donated all the lumber we'll need to make the stands," Mr. Collins told the group. "And he's dropping off a box of tools tomorrow afternoon as well."

"I can get a crew together to build the booths," Ken Matthews said.

Elizabeth scribbled in her notebook. "Regina, what would you like to do?" she asked.

Regina looked thoughtful. "I could organize all the refreshment stands," she suggested.

"I'll help with that," Enid volunteered.

"Now," Elizabeth said, consulting her list, "if Todd and Roger wouldn't mind taking charge of games, that covers just about everyone."

"What about me?" Winston demanded.

"You mean in addition to letting people throw pies at you?"

Everyone laughed, and Winston nodded.

Suddenly a flash of inspiration came to Elizabeth. "Winston, how would you like to be master of ceremonies? We'll need someone to direct people and announce prizes."

Winston looked delighted. "I'll borrow my father's old tuxedo," he said.

"OK," Elizabeth said, putting her notebook down. "It looks as though we're off to a good start. I'll arrange to meet with Mrs. Morrow, and we can meet again on Friday afternoon, if that's all right with everyone."

"Liz," Todd said, his brown eyes twinkling, "aren't you forgetting something?"

Elizabeth looked at him in confusion. "What do you mean?"

Todd laughed. "We're supposed to adjourn now to the beach!" he reminded her.

"That's right!" Enid cried.

Elizabeth laughed. "I *did* forget," she said. "Mr. Collins, how about a trip to the beach with the carnival committee?"

"No, thanks," Mr. Collins said. "You guys get out of here now and have a good time. I've got a little work to do."

"Thanks for all your help," Elizabeth told him as the group started out of the classroom. "It looks like this is going to take some work, but it'll sure be worth it if we can raise some money for those children."

"With you at the helm, Liz, I'm sure it'll be a roaring success." Mr. Collins chuckled. "Now go on and have a good time. It's too nice a day to waste inside!"

Half an hour later, Elizabeth, Enid, and Todd were lying on beach towels on the warm sand, listening to the waves crashing on the shore.

"Enid, where's George?" Elizabeth asked, rolling over on her stomach to face her friend.

George Warren was Enid's steady boyfriend,

and Elizabeth had just remembered he was supposed to meet them at the beach.

"He's at his junior flying class," she replied. "A thousand feet off the ground, as usual." For the past month or so, George had been trying to get his pilot's license, fulfilling a lifelong dream of learning to fly.

"I think I'd rather be on the ground on a day like this," Todd joked, rolling over on his back so his face could get some sun.

"I think the meeting went pretty well this afternoon," Enid commented a moment later. "I'm glad Ken Matthews is going to be helping. We need someone strong to build the booths!"

"I beg your pardon," Todd said, opening one eye. "And I suppose I'm nothing but a ninety-pound weakling?"

"You'll do," Elizabeth murmured, running her hand along the curve of his arm.

"Actually, I'm glad Ken will be around too," Todd remarked. "I thought he might miss the meeting this afternoon. I know how busy he's been with the election."

"That's right," Enid said. Ken was running for president of the Sweet Valley Centennial Student Committee, and he'd put a lot of effort into making posters and soliciting votes.

"Is anyone running against him yet?" Enid asked.

Todd shook his head. "It looks like Ken's got it

29

all wrapped up," he told her. "Like our friend Liz here—an uncontested victory."

"That's strange," Elizabeth said. Sweet Valley had been planning its centennial celebration for quite some time, and she would have expected the presidency of the student committee to be a coveted position. "I'll bet someone else signs up," she added, rubbing oil into her bronzed shoulders.

"Oh, yeah?" Todd said teasingly. "What would you like to bet, Elizabeth Wakefield?"

"A hot fudge sundae at the Dairi Burger," she told him.

"You're on!" Todd cried, grabbing her by the hand. "And I'll bet you an enormous kiss that I make it into the water before you do!"

"Jess, you should've seen this guy," Lila said, settling back on her enormous beach towel.

"Really? Where'd you find him?" Jessica asked, rummaging through her bag for a bottle of baby oil.

"I didn't *find* him," Lila said evasively, brushing a bit of sand off her tanned shoulder. "He was just—" She paused to think for a moment. "Just hanging around my father's office," she finished. She knew Jessica would be critical if she found out Jack was a construction worker. *Not that it matters*, Lila told herself. *At least, not that it matters yet.*

"So did you talk to this walking vision?" Jessica asked.

Lila nodded. "He's got a wonderful voice," she said. "And he really is pretty terrific looking."

"What's his last name?" Jessica asked.

Lila shrugged. "We didn't get around to that."

Jessica laughed out loud. "Oh, boy," she said. "Maybe it's Jack-in-the-box." She giggled. "Or Jack O'lantern. Or Jack the Ripper!"

"Shut up," Lila muttered, leaning forward to grab Jessica's baby oil. "He knows *my* last name. And I know I'll be seeing him again. I don't need his last name to find him!"

Jessica turned over on her stomach so she could watch people strolling back and forth in front of her. "Hey, where's Cara?" she asked, shading her eyes with one hand. "She was supposed to be here ages ago."

Lila sat up and looked around, her pretty face wrinkled in a frown. "God knows," she said. Suddenly her brown eyes narrowed. "Look who just arrived," she said to Jessica, pointing across the beach.

Jessica followed her gaze, her face darkening. Sure enough, there was Bruce Patman, tanned and muscular, in an absurdly small bathing suit. And right beside him, holding his hand as if she couldn't bear to let go of him for even a second, was Regina Morrow.

"They certainly look happy, don't you think?" Lila said brightly.

"Just give it time, Lila," Jessica said, rolling over on her back and closing her eyes. *Or give me time, I should say,* she thought. *There's no way I'm going to get stuck writing Lila's term paper. Whatever it takes, I'm going to make sure Bruce and Regina break up before the carnival.*

The only thing that remained was determining how to do it.

Four

"Roger, pass Regina the butter," Mrs. Patman said, smoothing her black hair with her hand.

Bruce glared at his mother across the table. "You don't have to treat Regina like a two-year-old," he had told her angrily while Regina was in the powder room washing her hands. "She may not be able to hear, but there's nothing wrong with her mind. Anyway, she can read lips perfectly."

"I'm sure she can," Mrs. Patman had said soothingly. But now, sitting at one end of the table in the Patmans' formidable dining room, she seemed to have forgotten everything Bruce had said. Each time she addressed Regina, she spoke very slowly and loudly, moving her lips with careful exaggeration. By the time one of the servants brought in the salad, Regina's face was red with embarrassment.

"That was such a lovely story about you in that little magazine," Mrs. Patman said loudly. "Wasn't it, dear?" she asked, looking down the table at her husband.

"Why are you shouting, Aunt Marie?" Roger asked, taking a bite of salad.

"Was I shouting? I wasn't shouting, was I?" Mrs. Patman demanded, turning with an injured look to Bruce.

"It *was* a lovely article," Mr. Patman said, smiling at Regina.

Blushing hotly, Regina stared down at her salad. Dinner was much harder than she'd expected. For one thing, the Patman mansion—though no larger than the Morrows' own—was imposing. Where the Morrows' house was warm and casual, the Patmans' was elegant and forbidding. *We could fit fifteen people at this table instead of five*, Regina thought to herself. An enormous chandelier hung over the dining room table, glinting in the candlelight. Regina thought the lighting was romantic, but it didn't make lip-reading very easy.

Still, as long as Bruce was across from her, smiling warmly and nudging her foot protectively with his under the table, Regina couldn't care less about the others. Regina thought Bruce looked more handsome than ever that evening. He was wearing a navy-blue blazer, chino pants, and a navy- and red-striped tie. *"You're* the one who belongs on the cover of a magazine," she had teased him when he'd come to pick her up earlier in the evening.

"Regina," Mrs. Patman said, twisting the heavy string of pearls around her neck, "I understand your mother has been put in charge of the carnival committee."

"Yes, ma'am," Regina said.

"I was rather hoping I would be asked to take that position," Mrs. Patman said haughtily.

"I think the PTA suggested my mother because she was new in town, and they thought she'd enjoy the opportunity to get involved," Regina said shyly. "And they knew she had experience with handicapped children. But I'm sure she'd be grateful for your help, Mrs. Patman. Mr. Fowler has already contributed lumber for the stalls."

"Oh, he has, has he?" Mrs. Patman asked, leaning back in her chair to consider this piece of news. Marie Patman hated the Fowlers. She hated them so much that she wasn't sure whether it was the *idea* of the Fowlers or the fact of them that so enraged her. According to Marie Patman, the Fowlers were nouveaux riches— newly rich. Not like the Patmans and the Vanderhorns, who were among the first families in Sweet Valley. Mrs. Patman leaned forward in her chair and smiled at Regina—her first real smile of the evening.

"Maybe I'll give your mother a call tonight and see what Henry and I can do to help," she said sweetly.

"I'm sure she'd be happy to hear from you," Regina said. *Mrs. Patman sure seems to run hot and cold*, she thought. But Bruce's smile across the table made everything worthwhile. "This soup is delicious, Mrs. Patman," she added, turning to her hostess with a smile.

"Do you think so, dear? I'm so glad," Mrs. Patman said happily, folding her hands together and beaming first at Regina and then at Bruce. Her voice had dropped back to normal, and she seemed to have forgotten that Regina was deaf. *Oh, well*, Regina thought to herself. *I guess I'm lucky that Bruce takes after his father. His mother really seems to have a few screws loose.*

"Your mother looked as if she was shouting at me the whole first half of the dinner," Regina said, sinking into Bruce's arms. They were parked in Bruce's Porsche at Miller's Point, a breathtaking spot overlooking Sweet Valley, watching the sun set.

Bruce laughed. "Try not to let my mother get to you," he said. "She means well, but she's got some pretty strange ideas."

"She really seemed to warm up after we started talking about my mother and the carnival committee," Regina pointed out.

Bruce shrugged. "She's crazy if it took her more than a minute to warm up to you," he said huskily, running his hands over Regina's silky hair.

Regina's breath caught in her throat. Bruce was the first boy who had touched her, and each time he held her, she felt almost dizzy with warmth.

Regina lay back in Bruce's arms, looking down at the sun setting over the valley. "It's so beautiful here," she murmured. She loved being alone with Bruce, away from everyone at home or at school, but her happiness was tinged with anxiety. *There's still so much I don't know*, Regina thought, closing her eyes as Bruce leaned over to kiss her. The feel of his lips on her throat made her sigh with happiness.

Suddenly Bruce pulled her up to face him. "I love you, Regina," he said softly, staring into her eyes. She stared back at him gravely and leaned forward to touch his lips with her fingers. How strange—how wonderfully strange—to see those words shaping themselves on Bruce's lips.

"I've never told any girl that I loved her before," he added seriously. "I want you to know that, Regina."

Regina blushed. "I've never even kissed a boy before," she admitted.

Bruce leaned over and tenderly—as tenderly as possible—kissed Regina on the earlobe. "I wish I could bring your hearing back with a kiss," he said softly, looking into her eyes. "You're so brave, Regina. If only there was something I could do so you could hear me tell you how much I love you!"

Regina smiled. "I'm not brave," she told Bruce quietly. "I'm happy. I have more now than I ever dreamed of having. For so many years I went to 'special' schools and 'special' camps and 'special' doctors. And it took me so long to adjust to the public school in Boston. Since I moved to Sweet Valley, I've been able to lead a normal life for the first time. And now there's you."

She pulled his face down to hers and kissed him softly on the lips. "I don't need to hear to know you love me," she whispered. "Or to know that I love you, too."

"Oh, Regina!" Bruce burst out. "What did I ever do before I met you?"

Regina shivered. It was hard to remember what life had been like before Bruce. The worst thing about her deafness was that it had isolated her from other people. Her family was wonderful—they always had been. But for years Regina had needed to be away from them so she could attend special schools. She had grown accustomed to being deaf and had come to take her handicap for granted. But it seemed her deafness had been a wall between her and other kids her age.

Bruce was the first person to break through that wall. And since she had met him, Regina felt like a different person. She wasn't isolated anymore. She could tell Bruce whatever she thought or felt, and he understood. Sometimes he even knew what she was thinking before she said anything.

"Nothing should ever keep us apart, Regina," Bruce said firmly, holding her head in his hands.

"Nothing will," Regina said, taking his hand and holding it tight. *Because I won't let it*, she thought. *Nothing in the whole world matters to me as much as Bruce does, and I won't let anything come between us. Not ever.*

Five

When Mrs. Patman called, Skye Morrow was in the living room, looking at a pile of notes Mr. Collins had given her to help her plan the carnival.

"What was that all about?" Mr. Morrow asked, taking his reading glasses off and putting down the evening paper after his wife had hung up the phone.

"The Patmans want to match the amount of money we raise at the carnival," Mrs. Morrow told him, rubbing her temples with both hands.

"That's pretty generous of them," Mr. Morrow said cheerfully. His wife stared at him unsmiling, and he wrinkled his brow with concern. "What's wrong, honey? I think that sounds like good news."

"I guess it is," Mrs. Morrow said. "But I didn't really like the way she sounded. She made it seem like some sort of contest to see who can give the most. And you should have heard the way she went on about how well Regina's adjusted to 'her little problem,' " she added indignantly. "She made it sound as though Regina's got two heads or something! And then she claims she wants to give hundreds of dollars to help the handicapped!"

"Skye," Mr. Morrow said gently, "those kids at the hospital aren't going to care where the money to help them out comes from. Even if it comes from a woman with two heads!" He chuckled.

Mrs. Morrow shook her head as she leaned back in her chair. "Maybe I should have trusted my impulses and told Roger Collins that I wasn't the right choice for supervising this project. I just can't seem to be objective about the whole thing."

"You'll be fine, Mom. You're exactly what they need," eighteen-year-old Nicholas Morrow said encouragingly.

Mrs. Morrow leaned over and rumpled his dark hair. "Thanks, handsome," she said, trying to smile. "I think I'll go upstairs and lie down for a while," she added, standing up and kneading her temples with both hands. "This project seems to be giving me a headache."

"I'm worried about Mom," Nicholas said after she had left the room. "She seems to be getting headaches again all the time now."

Mr. Morrow looked at his son and sighed. Sometimes he wished his son could remember Skye before Regina was born. As hard as he tried, it was impossible to convince Nicholas that his mother had once been a carefree, laughing young woman.

When Kurt Morrow met Skye, he was a professional football player, and she was a top fashion model who traveled on location all over the world. Sometimes Kurt had to pinch himself to prove he wasn't dreaming when she fell in love with him and agreed to marry him. They were a couple who had everything—looks, love, a perfect home, and a perfect little boy. After Kurt used his football earnings to start a computer business, Skye gave up modeling gradually, wanting to devote all her time to her husband, her home, and her son. Also, a new baby was on the way. And Skye was ready to be a full-time mother.

But a few weeks after she learned she was pregnant, one of the most glamorous magazines in New York offered her a spectacular assignment. They wanted Skye to appear in their special summer issue, modeling bathing suits and resort wear. After long discussions with Kurt, Skye decided to take the job. It would be her last modeling assignment, and she wanted it to be perfect.

There was only one catch. The magazine told her she would have to lose ten pounds in less than a month. Ignoring what her doctor told her, Skye took diet pills and lost the weight. The assignment went perfectly, and in the magazine's summer issue, Skye looked more beautiful than ever before.

But the consequences were grave. The pills Skye had taken had damaged the delicate tissue in the ears of her unborn child. After Regina was born, it became obvious that she wasn't responding to noises the way Nicholas had. The doctors' pronouncement was grave: Regina had suffered permanent damage to her ears. She would never be able to hear normally.

At first Skye refused to believe what the doctors told her. She wrote to clinics and hospitals all over the world, sending them Regina's medical files and begging them for help. Kurt had finally convinced her to accept the truth. Her children needed her now more than ever. Regina needed love from her mother, not guilt.

But Skye couldn't forgive herself. She gave up modeling completely, convinced that her work and her own selfishness had been to blame. In the past she had loved to entertain, but after Regina's condition was diagnosed, she spent more and more time alone with the children.

When Regina left home to attend a special boarding school in Connecticut, Skye began to suffer from blinding headaches. Sometimes they were so severe she couldn't leave her bed for days.

Mr. Morrow was aware that the headaches were caused by guilt and anxiety over Regina's deafness. Regina, of course, knew nothing about any of this. Whenever Regina was around, Mrs. Morrow made a special effort to act as if everything were fine.

When things went well for Regina, the headaches often stopped. Sometimes Skye felt like her old self. When Regina's picture appeared on the cover of *Ingenue*, Skye was as happy and excited as she had been in the days before Regina was born.

But over the past few weeks, Nicholas and Mr. Morrow had noticed a rapid change in her behavior. It was as if Skye had seen how close Regina could come to achieving what she herself had taken for granted. Now all the guilt and anxiety were back. Mr. Morrow sighed as he looked at the door through which his wife had disappeared. "I really hoped that moving here would make things better," he said softly. "At last we're all living together like a normal family."

Nicholas shook his head, his handsome face creasing with concern. "I don't know, Dad," he murmured. "I just wish there was something we could do!"

Mr. Morrow stood up and walked to the window, looking out at his estate as if he weren't really seeing what lay outside. "There *may* be something, son," he said at last. "I've been exploring some possibilities, and I think that now is the time to find out for sure." Without another word, he crossed the room, picked up the telephone receiver, and began to dial.

"Anyone home?" Regina called, closing the front door behind her and slipping out of her jacket. It was eleven-thirty, later than she'd thought, but the family room was still blazing with lights. *Looks like they're all still up*, she thought, hurrying to the back of the house. She could hardly wait to tell her mother about the evening. As she opened the door to the family room, she automatically reached to touch the tiny ruby pendant Bruce had given her the week before. She blushed as her fingers brushed the tiny jewel at her throat. *It's as if I don't really believe any of this can have happened*, she thought, smiling.

The scene that greeted her in the family room caught Regina by surprise. She had suspected that her mother hadn't been feeling well earlier, but Skye was still awake. And not only awake, but fully clothed, looking younger and more beautiful than ever before. Nicholas was pouring champagne into fluted glasses, and her father was smiling brightly.

"Hi!" Regina said, glancing from one happy face to the next. "What's the champagne for? Are we celebrating?"

"We certainly are!" her father boomed, coming forward and encircling Regina in his strong arms. "Nicholas, pour your sister a glass."

"Oh, Regina!" her mother cried, running forward and throwing her arms around her. "I'm so happy I could cry!"

"Wait a minute!" Regina stepped back and looked at all of them in confusion. "Can anyone explain what we're all so happy about?"

"We can indeed," her father said, reaching for a glass of champagne and passing it to Regina. "But first, I think we need a toast."

"To Regina," Mrs. Morrow said, her eyes filling with tears.

"To all of us," Nicholas added, raising his glass.

Regina laughed. "I'll drink to that," she said happily, sipping the delicious wine. She put her glass down and plopped down on the couch. "Now, what's going on?" she demanded.

Mr. Morrow took a deep breath. "Regina," he began, "what would you say if I told you there was a chance your hearing could be completely restored?"

Regina stared at him, her mouth going dry. "What?" she managed weakly.

Mr. Morrow nodded. "Completely, perfectly restored," he told her. "After approximately a year of treatments, you'll be able to hear as well as the rest of us. Concerts and birds singing and babies crying—"

And Bruce's voice telling me he loves me, Regina thought, closing her eyes in disbelief. "Are you serious?" she asked, opening her eyes and searching her father's face. "Is this some kind of joke?"

"Sweetie, do you think we'd joke about something like this?" her mother asked.

Regina stared at her and shook her head. "No," she said faintly. "It's just so hard to imagine," she added, a smile breaking across her face. "You mean there's really a doctor somewhere who thinks he can cure me?"

Mr. Morrow sat down on the couch next to his daughter and took her hand. "I would've told you months ago, but I didn't want to get your hopes up. Last year I read about a case similar to yours in which a boy from San Francisco had his hearing completely restored. I did as much research as I could and finally wrote to the doctor who invented the procedure. His name is Max Friederich. He's a brilliant Swiss surgeon. He answered several weeks later, telling me that the procedure could be used successfully only in about one case out of a thousand. Last month I had all your medical records sent to him. And tonight I got his colleague in New York City on the phone. He thinks that you're a perfect candidate for the treatment!"

Regina was trembling with excitement. The whole time her father was talking her mind was racing. *I'll be able to hear again*, she thought. *I'll hear Bruce's voice. I'll be able to talk to him on the telephone; and when we're together, I'll know what he's saying even with my eyes shut!* In her confusion and excitement, Regina could barely register what her father was telling her. All she knew was that he'd found a doctor who could make her hear again.

"We're going to come visit you, too," her mother was saying, laughing excitedly over her champagne glass. "We're not going to let this family be separated any more than we have to!"

"Come visit me where?" Regina asked blankly, turning back to her father. "Can't the procedure be done here in Sweet Valley?" A horrible, gnawing sensation began in the pit of her stomach. After a year of treatments, her father had said. A year! They couldn't expect her to go away for an entire year!

"Regina, Dr. Friederich is incredibly busy," her father told her. "We can't expect him to make house calls from Switzerland." Mr. Morrow was still laughing, unaware of the expression of growing horror on Regina's face.

"Switzerland!" she exploded. "You don't mean I'd have to move to Switzerland, do you?"

"Regina, it's only for a year," her mother said soothingly, putting her arms around her daughter. "You've been through so much already. One more year and you'll never have to worry again!"

"I'll come and visit you, Regina," Nicholas was saying eagerly. "We can go skiing together in the Alps."

"We'll *all* visit," Mr. Morrow said firmly. "And Dr. Friederich thinks you may be able to come home for two weeks at Christmas."

Regina looked from one excited face to another. "This procedure," she said slowly, trying not to burst into tears, "could it wait? Is there any reason why it has to be done right away?"

Mr. Morrow stared at her, his brow furrowing. "We thought you'd want to go as soon as you could," he told her. Obviously confused, he looked at his wife. "We'll arrange for a tutor so you can finish your schoolwork in Switzerland. But I suppose if you wanted to wait until school's out, we might try to reschedule with Dr. Friederich—if we can get you in then. He's a very busy man."

"What I meant," Regina said, "was waiting a little longer than that." She was still trembling, but she was no longer overflowing with joy.

Once again her fingers flew to her throat. The ruby pendant was still there.

"How *much* longer?" Mr. Morrow asked. "Regina, the operations should be done as soon as possible."

Regina jumped to her feet, her face blazing. "Forget it!" she cried, her eyes swimming with tears. "For the first time in my whole life, I've finally been able to live a normal life. I'm doing well in school. And I've made real friends! How can you expect me to just jump on a plane and spend the next year in a foreign country, with no one but doctors to talk to!"

Regina fought for control, but despite herself tears spilled over and trickled down her cheeks. "It's easy for *you*," she sputtered. "*You* can come visit and go skiing and then come home again! But I'm the one who has to make the decision. And I'm not going to go!"

Sobs bursting from her heaving chest, Regina ran from the room, slamming the door behind her. Her parents and Nicholas stared at one another, the color slowly draining from their faces.

Six

Regina stood in front of the mirror in her bedroom, brushing her long, black hair with automatic strokes. She examined herself critically, and, after a moment's deliberation, brushed a bit of blusher under each cheekbone. *That's better*, she thought, stepping back for a final look. She had chosen one of her favorite outfits to wear—a navy-blue cotton dress with tiny white flowers on it, and a pair of low-heeled sandals. Satisfied at last, Regina turned from the mirror. *It doesn't show*, she thought with relief. *You can't tell I've been crying or that I didn't get much sleep last night.*

Nicholas and Mr. Morrow were in the breakfast room when Regina went downstairs. They had apparently been talking about her because their lips stopped moving as soon as she walked in the room.

"Good morning," Regina said cheerfully, pouring herself a glass of milk and sitting down next to her brother. "Is Mom up yet?"

Mr. Morrow glanced anxiously at Nicholas and then cleared his throat. "She's not feeling very well this morning, Regina," he told her. "I think she's still pretty upset by what you said last night."

Regina's face became hot. "I owe you all a big apology," she said, taking a sip of milk. "I didn't behave very well last night. I guess I was too excited and then too upset to make very much sense."

Nicholas's face lit up. "You mean you've changed your mind?" he asked. "You want to go to Switzerland after all?"

Regina looked from Nicholas to her father. Both had the same hopeful expression, the same light in their eyes. Her heart melted when she saw them look at her that way. Regina knew how much they loved her, and she knew, too, that they genuinely wanted what was best for her. But she had made up her mind, and nothing would weaken her resolve. "I'm sorry," she said softly, staring down at the table. "I can't go," she added, looking up to meet her father's gaze. "If only you knew how happy I've been since we moved to Sweet Valley! For the first time in my life, I feel like a normal person."

"Regina, we know that," her father said. "And it's because we understand that we want you to undergo these treatments. Please think it over, Regina."

Regina sighed. "All right, I'll think it over," she agreed. "But I don't think I'll change my mind. Dad," she said, impulsively leaping up and throwing her arms around her father, "I know how much trouble you went through to find Dr. Friederich. And I love you for it. Please don't be angry with me if I decide to stay here in Sweet Valley."

Mr. Morrow hugged Regina. "You know we want what's best for you," he told her. "And it's not a question of being angry with you. We'll stick by you no matter what decision you come to. All we ask," he added firmly, "is that you keep an open mind about it, OK?"

"OK," Regina said softly. "That's fair enough."

The doorbell rang, and Nicholas jumped up to see who was there. "Oh, is that the door?" Regina asked. "That must be Bruce." She gave her father another kiss and hurried after Nicholas, her heart pounding. She didn't want Bruce to come inside that morning. And she didn't want Nicholas to get to him before she did.

* * *

"You look so beautiful this morning," Bruce said tenderly, kissing Regina softly before he started his Porsche in the Morrows' driveway.

"Thanks," Regina murmured, trying to keep her voice natural. She had promised herself the night before that Bruce would not find out about Dr. Friederich and Switzerland. *There's no point in letting him find out about it*, Regina thought. *Because no matter what Mom and Dad say, I know it would be wrong for me to go to Switzerland. I belong here.*

The whole time she was growing up, Regina had longed for the kind of life other girls took for granted. The special schools she had attended were a world away from Sweet Valley High. Tuition had been very expensive, and students had had to work twice as hard to accomplish the simplest tasks.

She had just felt comfortable in her first regular school, in Boston, when her father had announced they were moving to Sweet Valley. At first she had been worried about starting yet another school. She was afraid that no one would like her and that they would treat her differently. But week by week her confidence increased. It was easy now for Regina to do well in her schoolwork, and Sweet Valley High was quickly becoming a place to have fun as well as to learn.

For the first time in her life, Regina had a real circle of friends. She had a home she loved, and she had her family with her every single day. Sweet Valley had seemed almost magical to Regina since the day she moved in. And when Mr. Townsend had stopped her in the street and asked her if she'd like to model for a special story in *Ingenue* magazine, she *knew* it was magic.

But none of these things alone would have kept Regina from going to Switzerland. The prospect of sudden disruption and loneliness was difficult for her, but—to have her hearing restored! To be able to hear music and voices and rain falling on the rooftop at night! Where other people heard these things, all Regina could distinguish was a faint buzz.

Now, the choice was hers. The thing she had dreamed of for so many years had become a reality. She might hear again one day!

But now she had Bruce. And Bruce was the real reason why Regina knew she couldn't leave Sweet Valley. She had never dreamed that being in love could feel this way. She thought about Bruce every waking moment. The times when they couldn't be together seemed to drag on forever. *And*, Regina thought, *if a day without Bruce feels like a year to me, what would a year without him feel like?*

"Hey," Bruce said, leaning over and giving

her a hug with his free arm, "you're about a million miles away! What are you thinking about?"

Regina blushed. "I'm thinking how happy I am with you," she said shyly.

"Thank goodness," Bruce said, shaking his head. "Sometimes when you get quiet I start worrying that you may have changed your mind about me. It's funny," he added, pulling the Porsche into his usual parking place in the Sweet Valley High lot, "I never worried about a girl before. And now I'm worrying all the time!"

"There's nothing to worry about," Regina said. "You know that, don't you?"

Bruce sighed. "You're right," he said finally. "There's nothing to worry about as long as you tell me you haven't stopped caring about me. That's all that matters."

"Oh, Bruce," Regina cried, throwing her arms around him. *Thank goodness I didn't tell him about Switzerland*, she thought, breathing in the sweet smell of his after-shave. *He'd never understand. And if I were to lose him now, I'd be giving up the most precious thing of all.*

Millions of people in the world have perfect hearing, she reasoned. *But how many of them love someone with all their hearts who loves them back?*

Nothing can make me leave Sweet Valley and Bruce, she swore to herself, clinging to him as if she'd never let go. *Nothing—not even Dr. Friederich and his promise of a miracle.* And no matter what, Bruce was *not* going to learn about the treatments or her decision to forego them.

Because that's what loving someone means, Regina told herself. *It means, if you have to, you're willing to make a sacrifice for someone you really care about—like Bruce.*

"OK," Winston Egbert said cheerfully, "this is your lucky day! Your noontime meal is about to be graced with my humor and charm."

"Lucky us." Lila groaned. "Why are Jessica and I the fortunate ones today?"

"Good question," Winston said, sliding his tray next to Jessica's. "Actually, this is a business call," he added, taking a huge forkful of chocolate cake.

"You know, Winston," Lila commented, staring at his tray, "in this country, people generally eat dessert *after* the meal."

"A backward nation." Winston sighed. "I have come," he continued, gesturing grandly with his fork, "to invite you two to contribute your worthy ideas to the carnival committee."

"Carnivals are boring," Lila told him. "Besides," she added, "neither of us has time to help. We've both got these stupid term papers to worry about." She winked at Jessica.

What she means, Jessica thought glumly, *is that I've got both our stupid term papers to worry about.*

It didn't appear as though Bruce and Regina

were going to split up. In fact, they looked happier than ever. *It's enough to make a person nauseous, watching them carry on the way they do.* Bruce acted as though Regina were some kind of goddess or something.

"I'd be delighted to help you guys, Winston," Jessica said impulsively, her blue-green eyes flashing defiantly at Lila. "After all, it's silly to spend all my time in the library."

"A brilliant conclusion!" Winston declared, swallowing the last bite of cake. "Now for dessert, we have a tasty hamburger," he explained to Lila, picking his burger up with a flourish. "What kind of booth would you like to take charge of?" he asked Jessica.

"I don't know yet," Jessica said grimly, watching Bruce and Regina leave the cafeteria with their arms locked around each other.

Lila followed her gaze and turned to Winston, a malicious smile playing about her lips. "Maybe Jess should have a black magic booth!" She got up from the table and picked up her tray. "You may need some magic soon," she told Jessica. "Nothing else seems to be working!"

"What's she talking about?" Winston asked, staring after Lila as she walked away.

"Nothing," Jessica said grimly, leaning back in her chair. *Lila hasn't won the bet yet*, she told herself, chewing idly on the end of her straw. *And if she thinks I'm going to give in without a struggle, she's got another think coming!*

I wonder if I've got the time wrong, Elizabeth thought, pressing the Morrows' doorbell for the third time. *I could have sworn Mrs. Morrow said four o'clock.*

She could hear the bell echoing inside the Morrows' magnificent home, but still no one answered. "Oh, well," Elizabeth said softly, turning down the walk. "Maybe she was called away suddenly and couldn't get in touch with me."

"Elizabeth?" she heard a voice call. Spinning around, Elizabeth saw Regina's mother standing in the doorway.

"I'm sorry," Elizabeth said, hurrying up the front walk again. "I thought you weren't home."

Mrs. Morrow shook her head, her dark hair tumbling, uncombed, around her shoulders. "I was sleeping," she said flatly. "I haven't been feeling well, so I asked all the servants to leave. Come in, please," she added. "I'll put a kettle on and make us some tea."

Elizabeth looked at Mrs. Morrow with concern. "Are you feeling all right?" she asked anxiously, noticing the blue circles under Mrs. Morrow's eyes and the pained expression on her face.

"I'm all right," Mrs. Morrow replied, leading

Elizabeth through the plant-filled foyer to the sunny breakfast room. "I think some tea may help," she added, looking vaguely around as if she didn't know where she was.

"Please, Mrs. Morrow, sit down," Elizabeth urged. "I'll make tea."

To her surprise, Mrs. Morrow obeyed, sinking into the nearest chair and putting her face in her hands. "I'm sorry," she said weakly. "I should have called and canceled our appointment. But I completely forgot about the carnival."

Elizabeth went into the kitchen and put a kettle of water on the stove. Mrs. Morrow's appearance had really disturbed her. Her beautiful face had been tear-streaked, her fingers trembling as she kneaded her brow.

When Elizabeth came into the breakfast room carrying a tray with the teapot, cups, sugar, and milk, Mrs. Morrow looked up at her. "I'm sorry, Elizabeth. I hate letting anyone see me this way," she said softly. "But I get these terrible headaches."

"How often do the headaches come?" Elizabeth asked gently, pouring Mrs. Morrow a cup of hot tea. "Regina never said a word about them."

Mrs Morrow looked horrified. "You mustn't tell Regina," she said anxiously. "Promise me you won't tell her, Elizabeth."

Elizabeth sat down across from Mrs. Morrow.

"Of course not," she said softly. "If you don't want me to, I won't say a word to anyone. Have you seen a doctor?"

Mrs. Morrow nodded as she took a tiny sip of tea. "Thank you, dear," she said, setting the cup down again. "It's delicious. Yes," she added with a bitter laugh. "I've seen a doctor. About a dozen of them, in fact. And they all say the same thing. There's nothing wrong with me."

"I don't understand—" Elizabeth began.

Mrs. Morrow cut her off. "It's Regina," she said quietly. "I haven't felt the same since Regina was born. You see, Elizabeth, her deafness is my fault." And, taking a deep breath, she told Elizabeth the whole story, right up to the previous night and Regina's shocking outburst.

"Oh, dear," Elizabeth said, leaning back in her seat. "So Regina positively refuses to go to Switzerland?"

Mrs. Morrow nodded helplessly. "Elizabeth, do you think you could try to change her mind?" she cried. "I know how much Regina admires you."

Elizabeth bit her lip. What should she say? On the one hand, she believed Regina was making a mistake. From what Mrs. Morrow had told her, it didn't sound as though Regina had mentioned Bruce to her parents when she told them she couldn't leave Sweet Valley. But Elizabeth was convinced Bruce had a great deal to do with Regina's decision.

And try as she might to give Bruce the benefit of the doubt, Elizabeth still didn't trust him. How could Regina throw away so much for his sake? Even though Elizabeth would never betray her friend by telling her mother about Bruce, Elizabeth felt she owed it to Regina to intervene.

On the other hand, Elizabeth hated to interfere. This was a big decision, and it seemed like one that only Regina could make.

"I don't know what I can do," Elizabeth said carefully, not wanting to upset Mrs. Morrow further. "But if Regina comes to me for advice, I'll certainly do what I can to persuade her to go ahead with the operations."

"Oh, Elizabeth, thank you," Mrs. Morrow said gratefully. "We're going to do our best to change her mind," she added. "There's a boy in San Francisco who was successfully treated by Dr. Friederich last year, and we've invited him to come down this weekend to meet Regina. Maybe *he* can convince her."

"I hope so," Elizabeth said slowly. Privately, she had her doubts. Regina had fallen in love for the first time, and she'd fallen pretty hard. Elizabeth didn't think anything short of a miracle would convince Regina to leave Bruce now—however much she had to give up to stay.

Seven

"Eight days till that stupid carnival," Jessica grumbled, stretching her long legs in front of her on the lawn. It was Friday afternoon, and Jessica was sitting on the grassy slope in front of Sweet Valley High, waiting for her friend Cara Walker to emerge. Cara had said one of the shops in town had a swimsuit sale on, and Jessica had agreed to go with her to see what they had.

I wish she'd hurry up, Jessica thought grumpily. Sweet Valley High wasn't her favorite place to spend a sunny late afternoon—particularly on a Friday!

"Hi, Jess," a friendly voice called. "What are you doing here?"

"Oh, hi, Ken," Jessica said, shading her eyes

63

and squinting up at Ken Matthews. "I'm waiting for Cara," she said irritably. "If she's not out here in another minute, I'm going to leave."

Ken sighed, plopping down beside her on the grass. "Sounds like your mood's about as good as mine right now," he muttered, picking a blade of grass.

"Why? What's wrong with you?" Jessica asked, more out of habit than real interest. Right then Jessica couldn't care less why he was in a bad mood. All she could think about was her bet with Lila.

"It's Bruce Patman," Ken said moodily, tearing the blade of grass into little bits. "It figures he'd suddenly decide he wants to run for president of the centennial committee. The election's only a week away, and out of the blue he decides he's going to run against me!"

"No one will vote for Bruce," Jessica said automatically. "I'm sure you'll win anyway, Ken."

Ken shook his head. "I doubt it. You know the Patmans. They take things like this seriously! They'll probably hire him a campaign manager and buy him television time so he can advertise!"

Jessica couldn't believe anyone cared that much about being president of the student centennial committee, but it seemed rude to say so to Ken.

"Wait and see," she said instead, wishing Ken

64

would go away so she could scheme in peace. "I'll bet you still win."

Ken sighed. "I don't think so, Jess. Besides," he pointed out, "Bruce is much more popular now that he's going out with Regina. You should hear the way people talk about him! They act like he's undergone some sort of overnight transformation. He's bound to win now," he concluded bitterly. "And I'm sure he doesn't really even want to be president. He probably just threw his name in for the hell of it."

Jessica stared at Ken, her mind racing. He had just given her a wonderful idea! Ken thought Bruce was much more popular since he'd met Regina. What if Jessica could convince Regina that was the only reason he'd gotten involved with her? If she could make it seem as if this election really mattered to Bruce—one his family insisted he win—and that he'd planned to run even before he met Regina . . .

It just might work, Jessica thought, jumping to her feet. It was a long shot, but she was getting desperate. "I just remembered something," she told Ken, grabbing her jacket. "I have to meet Liz at home."

"What about Cara?" Ken asked, watching Jessica bound for the bus stop.

"Tell her I just remembered an urgent meeting!" Jessica called. *I think it's about time*, she thought, *that I really do get involved with the carni-*

val committee. It's the best way I can think of to spend some time alone with Regina.

And after all, she thought, searching through her bag for the bus fare, *it's such a worthwhile cause!*

"It looks like our committee is shrinking," Winston pointed out, shaking the water from his hair like a wet puppy.

Elizabeth, Todd, Olivia, and Winston were in the Wakefield backyard, surrounded by piles of paper.

"Winston," Elizabeth said, laughing, "you're getting our notes all wet."

"How could I resist your swimming pool on a day like this?" Winston demanded, looking injured.

"Where's Ken?" Todd asked. "We really *are* dwindling," he added.

"He said he'd try to make it later," Olivia told them. "I think he's trying to come up with a new campaign strategy, now that he has a candidate to compete with."

"I don't know how we can stand all the excitement," Winston said. "Political intrigue comes at last to Sweet Valley High."

"What do you think Bruce's chances are?" Todd asked curiously. "I wouldn't have thought he'd have much of a shot against Ken."

"Me either," Elizabeth agreed. "Ken seems the perfect candidate to me."

Olivia looked thoughtful. "I'm not sure. I know what you two think of Bruce," she said, looking at Elizabeth and Todd, "but he really does seem to have changed since he met Regina. I think he'd do a good job."

Elizabeth sighed. She had seen the way he treated Jessica, and she couldn't believe he could change so quickly. And since her talk with Regina's mother, she liked him even less. *I bet Bruce couldn't care less even if he knows why Regina isn't going to Switzerland*, she thought angrily.

"I don't know, Liv," Todd said mildly. "Regina's a terrific girl, and I'm sure Bruce has been softened just by being around her. But—"

"Once a jerk, always a jerk," Winston filled in.

Olivia laughed. "I don't blame you guys for being skeptical," she told them. "But if I were you, I'd give Bruce a chance. People *can* change," she pointed out.

Todd grinned. "Maybe you're right, Olivia," he said. "If anyone could turn a toad into a prince, it would be Regina."

Elizabeth sighed. "I hate to change the subject," she told them, "but if we're going to have a carnival a week from tomorrow, we'd better get to work."

"Hey," Winston interrupted, "look who's here!"

Jessica flung herself down at the table and wiped her brow dramatically. "Liz," she cried. "Am I too late?"

"It depends." Elizabeth giggled. "Too late for what?"

"I've got a brilliant idea for the carnival," Jessica gasped.

"In that case," Todd said and grinned, "you're just in time. What's your idea, Jess?"

"Well," Jessica began, still out of breath, "what about a mother-daughter fashion show? We would set it up in one corner of the tent or get a smaller tent for it, and charge people a dollar for tickets."

Elizabeth frowned thoughtfully. "Not bad," she mused. "Do you think Mom would do it?"

Jessica burst out laughing. "Not *me*, Liz," she said, giggling. "And you think *I'm* vain," she added.

Elizabeth blushed. "Well, who did you have in mind?" she asked her twin.

"Regina and her mother, of course," Jessica replied. "It's perfect. Regina has appeared in *Ingenue* already, and her mother used to be a model in New York."

"It's a great idea, Jess," Elizabeth said carefully, "but I'm not sure Mrs. Morrow would agree to do it."

"Oh, I can convince her," Jessica said airily.

"I don't know." Elizabeth sighed. Much as she

loved her twin, she occasionally doubted Jessica's tact. And she knew how delicate things were between Regina and her mother right then. Sending Jessica over to the Morrow household would hardly be helpful.

"Well, I'm going to try," Jessica insisted. "Honestly, Liz. How do you expect to organize a big event like this unless you're willing to take some chances?"

"OK, OK," Elizabeth said. "Go ahead, Jess. Do your worst." *Mother-and-daughter modeling show*, she wrote in her notebook, putting a big question mark beside the entry.

I'm sure Regina and Mrs. Morrow can refuse Jessica better than I can, she thought, lifting her pencil and turning to Todd. "I just hope setting Jessica loose on them won't be too terribly unfair!"

"Thanks for the ride," Regina said softly, kissing Bruce on the cheek. "What time are you coming by tonight?"

"How about seven-thirty?" Bruce asked her, getting out of the car to open the door on her side.

"Seven-thirty," Regina said, leaning forward to kiss his lips, "is perfect. I'll see you then."

She watched as he drove around the circular driveway and turned down the road to the Patman estate, waving after him. Then she walked slowly to the front door. The last few days had been very awkward around the Morrow household, and Regina could feel her steps slowing as she wondered what she would find inside.

Regina had stuck to her decision, and she could tell how worried and upset by it her parents were. Her mother, in particular, didn't seem herself. But whenever Regina asked her what was wrong she just looked sad. Even Nicholas had been unusually withdrawn.

"Regina!" Nicholas called now, hurrying forward to meet her. "Come out to the backyard for a minute. There's someone here I want you to meet."

Her curiosity rising, Regina followed her older brother out to the expansive backyard shaded by thick trees. A boy was lying in the hammock, a book in his hand. He clambered to his feet when he saw Regina.

"This is Donald Essex," her brother told her. "He's come down from San Francisco to spend the weekend with us."

"Hello," Regina said shyly, putting out her hand.

Donald looked about the same age as Nicholas. He had thick, sandy hair and green eyes.

To her surprise, he greeted her in sign language, the international language of the deaf.

"Are you deaf, too?" she asked him, puzzled.

Donald laughed. "I was," he told her. Something about his frank, easy manner made Regina warm to him at once. "But I'm not anymore. Remember the boy your parents told you was cured by Dr. Friederich last year?"

Regina stared at him. "You're the one?" she asked, astounded. "What are you doing here?"

"Your parents invited me down for the weekend." Donald grinned. "I guess I'm a surprise—a good one, I hope."

"I'll leave you two to get better acquainted," Nicholas said cheerfully. "Watch out for him, though, Regina. He plays a mean game of Frisbee."

Regina's heart melted as she watched her brother stroll across the lawn. How wonderful her family was! They had invited Donald down hoping he could change her mind. *If only there was some way I could convince them that I'm really happier as I am*, she thought regretfully. *If they knew that, maybe they'd stop worrying.*

"How about a game of Frisbee?" Donald asked her.

"No, thanks," Regina said, smiling. "From what Nicholas just said, I don't think I'd have much of a chance."

"Well, how about a walk, then? This area is beautiful."

"Sure," Regina said, falling in step beside him. She couldn't help staring at Donald. How did it

71

feel to be able to hear again after being deaf? she wondered.

Within minutes she and Donald were talking as if they'd known each other for years. Like Regina, Donald had spent a good part of his childhood in special schools. He, too, had felt isolated and he had worked incredibly hard to win acceptance at a public high school in San Francisco. "I even tried out for the swim team," he told her, laughing. "And I did pretty well on it, too."

Regina couldn't believe it when she glanced down at her watch and saw it was almost six o'clock. "I'm sorry," she told Donald, "but we'd better turn back. I have to grab a bite to eat and take a quick shower. I have a date tonight," she added.

Donald smiled. "We'll have more time to talk tomorrow," he told her. "Don't worry, Regina," he added. "I'm not going to pressure you. That isn't why I came down here. I may not understand what you're going through, but I know it's a rough decision to make. You know," he added, "some people are more afraid of what comes *after* the treatments than the treatments themselves. They've gotten used to being deaf. Or, in some cases, they're afraid of the thought of hearing. They're afraid of what it would mean to be 'normal' all of a sudden."

Regina flushed deeply. "Donald, I'm not

afraid," she told him quietly. "If I had only myself to think of, I'd be on the first plane to Switzerland I could find." Her eyes filled with tears. How could everything be so confusing suddenly?

"We'll talk tomorrow," Donald said, squeezing her shoulder lightly.

Despite her love for her parents and her sympathy with their desire to do what was best for her, Regina was beginning to feel as if she were being pulled in two directions at once. And the tension was becoming unbearable. *It's got to get easier around here*, she thought miserably. *Sooner or later they'll forget all about Switzerland, and life will go back to normal—won't it?*

Eight

"Liz, what are you doing in there? I need to use the phone!" Jessica wailed, pounding on her sister's closed door with both fists.

"I'm working on the carnival," Elizabeth called, her voice muffled. "Why don't you use the extension in your room?"

"I can't find it," Jessica replied, opening the door and cheerfully barging in. "It's buried somewhere."

"I bet it is," Elizabeth said, laughing. "Come on, Jess—can't you see I'm busy?"

"Don't worry, Liz," Jessica said, picking up the phone and beginning to dial. "It's carnival business, anyway."

"As long as you're quick," Elizabeth mumbled, distracted.

But Jessica got Elizabeth's attention when she said into the phone, "Hello, is Regina there?" Elizabeth shot her a look. Jessica's cheeks turned bright red. "Oh, how thoughtless of me, Mrs. Morrow," she said quickly. "Of course she can't."

Elizabeth shook her head in disbelief. *Only my twin*, she thought, *would ask to speak to a deaf girl on the phone. It just figures.*

"Oh, dear. Well, actually, Mrs. Morrow, I wanted to speak to you as well as Regina. It's Jessica Wakefield calling."

"Of course," Mrs. Morrow said over the phone. "Can I give Regina a message? She's outside right now with a friend of ours."

"Well, I was wondering if I could drop by in about a half hour," Jessica said. "I wanted to talk to both of you about the carnival."

"I don't see why not," Mrs. Morrow said. "We're all going out later this afternoon, but if you come by fairly soon, you should catch us. I'll let Regina know you're coming."

"And to think I worried about your putting your foot in your mouth," Elizabeth said wryly when Jessica had replaced the receiver.

"I forgot about it for a minute, that's all," Jessica said defensively. "Actually, it's a compliment to Regina. She acts so much like the rest of us that I forgot she wouldn't be able to hear me on the phone."

Elizabeth laughed. "Jess, if you can convince the Morrows to do this modeling show, I'll clean your room," she promised.

"Don't worry," Jessica told her, glancing quickly in the mirror and charging out of the room. Jessica didn't care whether Regina modeled at the carnival or not. What mattered was making sure Regina understood that Bruce had been using her all along. It was going to take some careful planning to carry this off, but Jessica hadn't felt this good in days. *If anyone can botch up a perfect relationship,* she thought, grinning, *it's me. And right now, the stakes are high enough to make sure I give this mission all I've got!*

Regina was sitting outside on a deck chair, trying to read while Nicholas and Donald played badminton. It was a gorgeous day—too gorgeous, in fact, to concentrate on the book she was reading. She sighed, laying it face down on the table beside her. The sun caught her wrist as she moved, flashing brilliant colors through the small diamond on the bracelet Bruce had given her the previous night.

Every time Regina looked at the bracelet her face flushed. She remembered Bruce's expression as he had fumbled with the clasp, trying to put it on her wrist. "Bruce, this must have cost a fortune," she had whispered.

Bruce shook his head, his expression serious.

"Sometimes I don't think you realize how I feel about you, Regina," he had murmured. He kissed her softly then, his lips warm and gentle.

Regina had just stared at him, absolutely speechless. After Bruce had taken her home, she lay awake in bed and realized that the confusion she had been feeling that week was misguided. "This is where I belong," she whispered, turning over and pushing her face into the pillow. "As long as Bruce is here, I'm not going anywhere!"

Mrs. Morrow came out to the patio and tapped Regina on the shoulder. "Jessica Wakefield is here."

"Hi, Jess!" Regina said, sitting up and swinging her legs over the side of the chair.

"Can I get you something cold to drink?" Mrs. Morrow asked. "How about some iced tea?"

"No, thanks," Jessica said brightly. "I'm not going to stay long. I just came to ask you both if you'd be willing to do a special booth at the carnival. Liz is kind of worried," she added on impulse. "She's afraid things won't get organized in time."

"Oh, dear," Mrs. Morrow said, sitting down on a deck chair. "I'm afraid that may be my fault. What can we do to help?"

"Well," Jessica said, "how would you feel about a mother-daughter fashion show? Olivia Davidson says we can get a special tent from her uncle that we could set up near the big one. And

I can arrange to get some clothes for you two from Lisette's."

Regina looked quickly at her mother. She was sure she'd refuse. Her mother hated being reminded of her former career, and Regina was certain she'd never consent to modeling clothes in front of so many people.

"What do you think, Regina?" her mother asked slowly.

Regina stared at her. "Do you mean you'd actually do it?" she asked.

Mrs. Morrow shrugged. "Why not?" she replied. "It sounds like fun. Besides," she added, looking directly at Regina, "it's for a very good cause."

Jessica smiled. "Elizabeth will be so happy," she told them. "I can guarantee you'll draw a big crowd!"

Mrs. Morrow stood up, looking past Jessica out into the backyard. "Where have the boys gone?" she asked Regina. "I wanted to see if they could use some iced tea."

"I don't know," Regina told her. "They were playing badminton about ten minutes ago. Maybe they're out front."

"I'll leave you two, then, and see if I can find them," Mrs. Morrow said.

"Regina," Jessica exclaimed, leaning forward and staring at her wrist. "Where in the world did you get that gorgeous bracelet?"

Regina flushed. "Bruce gave it to me last night," she said softly.

Good Lord, Jessica thought. *Bruce has really gone completely mad. He'll probably thank me one day for saving his bank account.*

"You're really crazy about Bruce, aren't you?" Jessica asked innocently.

Regina nodded. "He's so wonderful, Jess," she said. "I don't think I've ever been so happy."

Jessica shook her head, her blond hair tumbling over her tanned shoulders. "It just goes to show," she murmured. "You should never listen to rumors."

"Rumors?" Regina asked, her face wrinkling in confusion. "What rumors?"

Jessica shrugged. "Don't give it another thought," she said. "People can be so stupid, Regina. The minute they see a really happy couple—like you and Bruce—they get jealous and start suggesting the most idiotic things."

Regina looked completely baffled. "What have people been saying about Bruce and me?" she demanded.

Jessica waved her hand. "Forget I even brought it up," she insisted. "They're all complete fools. It's obvious you and Bruce are perfect for each other."

Regina pleated the material of her shorts anxiously, her blue eyes darkening. "Really, Jess," she said firmly. "I want to know."

Jessica sighed. "All right," she yielded. "But remember, Regina, it's all complete nonsense."

Regina nodded, staring dumbly at Jessica as she spoke.

"It all has to do with this ridiculous election," Jessica began. "I'm sure Bruce told you all about it ages ago."

"What election?" Regina demanded.

Jessica's brow wrinkled with surprise. "Oh, didn't he tell you about it? Hmmm," she murmured. "That's strange."

"Jessica, what are you talking about?" Regina cried.

Jessica shook her head. "I'm sure it doesn't mean a thing," she said doubtfully. "You see, Bruce is running against Ken Matthews for president of the Sweet Valley Centennial Student Committee. *I* think it's a pretty silly position, but you know the Patmans. They care so much about being in charge of every last thing around here, I'm sure they pushed Bruce into it."

"But what does that have to do with me?" Regina asked, looking more confused than ever.

Jessica shrugged. "Probably not a thing," she assured her. "Regina, just forget I brought the whole thing up. It's so stupid."

Regina's face darkened. "Jessica, *please* tell me," she begged. "I can't stand having people say things about me behind my back."

"All right." Jessica sighed. "Ken Matthews is

really angry that Bruce is running against him. *He* says that Bruce wouldn't stand a chance of winning if it weren't for you. Since you two started going out, Bruce has gotten so much more popular. I guess you can sort of see Ken's point," Jessica concluded vaguely.

Regina stared at her. "I don't think I really understand," she said. "You mean people think Bruce has only been dating me so more people would vote for him in this election?"

Jessica nodded. "I told you it was absurd," she replied.

Regina laughed. "It sure is," she said, visibly relieved. "It's completely absurd."

"Of course," Jessica said thoughtfully, toying with her lavaliere, "it *is* kind of strange that Bruce didn't mention the election to you. He probably just forgot," she said brightly.

"Probably," Regina said, her voice firmly suggesting that she'd heard enough. "I'm glad you came over, Jess. The fashion show sounds like it'll be a lot of fun."

"Good," Jessica said, getting to her feet. "You two will be fabulous together. I'll get back to you later on with details," she added.

"Let me walk you to your car," Regina said, standing up as well.

Jessica wouldn't hear of it. "Stay right where you are and finish your book," she insisted. "I'll just walk around the side of the house." *And leave you alone to start wondering if there's a grain of truth in what I told you*, she added silently.

And Lila thought I needed black magic, Jessica thought, a tiny smile on her face as she hurried toward the Morrows' driveway.

"Damn!" Jessica muttered, turning the key in the ignition of the Fiat for the third time and waiting for the engine to start. Generally the car was reliable, but it seemed to be temperamental that day. Jessica was sitting in the Morrows' driveway, her pretty face screwed up with irritation. "I hate this car," she muttered, pumping the gas pedal with all her might.

"Don't flood the motor," a cheerful voice advised.

Jessica looked up with surprise. A tall, sandy-haired boy was standing beside her, resting his hands on the hood of the car. He smiled winningly, his green eyes shining.

Jessica blushed. "It doesn't seem to work," she said helplessly. "What should I do?"

"Get out," he said, laughing. "I'll see what I can do."

"My name is Jessica," she said, climbing out of the car. "Do you live around here?"

He laughed again, getting into the driver's seat. "My name is Donald Essex," he told her. "Nice to meet you, Jessica. And to answer your question—no," he said, starting the car on the first try. "I'm from San Francisco. I'm staying with the Morrows for the weekend." He got out of the car, and Jessica slid back into the driver's seat.

"Too bad you're not staying longer," Jessica said, flashing him her prettiest smile. "You're going to miss our carnival."

"What carnival?" Donald asked.

Jessica laughed. "If you decide to stick around for a while, give me a call and I'll tell you about it," she said. "Regina has my number."

"Wait a minute!" Donald cried. But Jessica, relying on a delicate sense of timing acquired through years of practice, put her foot on the gas pedal and roared around the driveway.

Not a bad morning, she thought, grinning. *I've convinced Regina and her mother to model at the carnival. I've met a mysterious out-of-towner with a fabulous smile.*

And above all, she reminded herself, *I've done what I could to start trouble between Bruce and Regina.* The rest, she figured, she'd have to leave up to the happy couple.

Nine

Regina woke up early Sunday morning. The whole house was still sleeping, and for a minute, before her mind had really cleared, she didn't know exactly what was wrong. She stretched languorously, and her gaze fell on the bracelet she had placed on the night table next to her bed. Then Regina remembered.

Everything Jessica had said the day before came flooding back to her, word for word. *It's ridiculous to distrust Bruce*, she reminded herself. *As soon as I see him again, everything will be all right. I'm only worried because I didn't see him last night.*

But Regina couldn't help feeling uneasy. She got up and dressed quickly, putting on a pair of white cotton jeans and a striped T-shirt. Crossing back to her night table, she fastened the bracelet around her wrist. Bruce was supposed to come by around noon. They were going on a picnic, and as soon as she talked to him about this silly election, she'd know nothing was wrong.

And nothing is wrong, she told herself. *Nothing at all.*

When she went downstairs, Donald was pouring himself a cup of coffee in the breakfast room. "You're up early," Regina said, surprised.

Donald laughed. "It's a carry-over from my year in Switzerland, I think," he told her. "I used to wake up before the sun rose there. Now I feel really lazy if I stay in bed after nine."

Regina took the coffee he offered her and sat down with him at the table, stirring milk and sugar into her cup.

Donald whistled softly. "Where'd you get that?" he asked her, brushing her bracelet with his finger.

Regina stared down at the table. "From a friend," she told him.

Donald smiled. "It must be a pretty special friend," he commented.

Regina smiled shyly at Donald. She liked him. Already he felt like an older brother to her, and she knew she could trust him. "It is," she admitted, taking a sip of her coffee. "A really special friend."

Regina got up to get some bread for toast. While she was popping the slices into the toaster, Donald asked her about Sweet Valley High and how she liked living in Southern California. While they ate, they exchanged memories of the transition from "special" to "normal" schools. Donald had one hilarious story after another about his high school in San Francisco, and once again Regina marveled at how comfortable she felt with him.

"This may be none of my business," Donald said awkwardly, leaning back in his chair, "but does this special friend have anything to do with your decision not to go to Switzerland?"

Regina flushed. She didn't know what to say. But Donald seemed to understand that it was hard for her to answer.

"Would you mind if I told you another story?" he continued.

"Go ahead." Regina smiled and took another sip of coffee.

He looked at her very seriously, and after a moment he began. "When I found out about Dr. Friederich's treatment I decided not to go ahead with it. That may surprise you, since I've been advocating your going ahead with the whole thing. But at the time I didn't want to leave San Francisco. You see, I'd just met a girl, and I couldn't bear the thought of leaving her."

Donald paused. "Do you want to hear the rest of this?"

"Yes," Regina said, her eyes steady on his. "Go ahead."

"Her name was Rosemary," Donald added. "She was a year older than I was and had already started college. But I saw her every weekend, and I knew if I moved to Switzerland I wouldn't see her at all. Not until Christmas, anyway. Well, I decided not to tell her about the treatments. I was afraid she'd tell me to go ahead with them. Eventually she *did* find out. But her reaction wasn't what I expected. She said she didn't want to see me anymore. She was furious that I hadn't trusted her enough to let her in on my decision. And that was that."

"So you went to Switzerland," Regina finished for him.

Donald nodded. "I wrote her several times. I was hoping she'd just staged the whole breakup so I'd go. But she wasn't that sort of girl. She meant what she said, and she stuck to it."

Regina sighed. She wished she could confide in Donald, but it didn't feel right to talk about Bruce behind his back. And though she was sorry about Donald and Rosemary, she couldn't help feeling that things were different with her and Bruce. Even if Bruce begged her to go, she couldn't bear to be without him for a whole year.

Unless, she thought uneasily, *what Jessica told me yesterday is true*.

"Regina," Donald said suddenly, "this procedure changed my whole life. I know I shouldn't interfere with your decision, but I know what you're going through, and I can't bear to see you make this kind of mistake! Promise me you'll think the whole thing through before you definitely say no."

"I promise," Regina said, and she meant it. Donald was right. This was a big decision she was making, and she owed it to everyone—especially herself—to give it serious consideration.

The first step, she thought, *is to have a long talk with Bruce*. Regina was sure Jessica had misunderstood. If Bruce was really running for president of the centennial committee, he would have told Regina about it.

Unless, she thought miserably, *there's some reason he doesn't want me to know*.

"Regina, is anything wrong?" Bruce asked, driving his car around the Morrows' driveway. "You've been awfully quiet all afternoon."

Regina sighed and pulled her long black hair off her neck with both hands. Bruce was right; she *had* been quiet. The picnic had been beautiful, but Regina couldn't relax. She wasn't very hungry, either. At one point she had steered the conversation to the subject of school and the carnival committee, giving Bruce a perfect chance to mention running for centennial president, but he hadn't responded. Even when she'd mentioned Ken Matthews, he hadn't taken the bait.

"Didn't you have a good time this afternoon?" he asked her now, parking his Porsche in front of the Morrows' mansion.

"I had a wonderful time, Bruce," Regina murmured. "It's just . . ."

"Just what?" Bruce urged, taking her hand and entwining her slender fingers with his own. "What is it, Regina? There's something bothering you. I can tell."

"Bruce," Regina began tentatively, "somebody told me something the other day about your running for president of the centennial committee. And I told them you weren't, since you hadn't mentioned it to me. You're *not* running, are you?"

Bruce thought for a minute. "Who told you that?" he asked at last.

"What difference does that make?" Regina cried, her face reddening. So maybe it *was* true!

"I don't really want to talk about it," Bruce said, shrugging. *It was supposed to be a surprise for Regina when I won*, he thought. *I could just kill whoever told her.*

"Why not?" Regina demanded. "And why didn't you mention it to me to begin with?"

"I just don't want to talk about it," Bruce said firmly. He felt a little uneasy about the whole thing. He had a feeling Ken Matthews was going to win, and he didn't want Regina to feel terrible if things worked out that way. No, better to brush the whole thing off now, keep it from turning into a big deal.

But Regina's eyes were darkening with anger as Bruce stared at the cover on his steering wheel. *I never would have believed this in a million years*, she thought furiously, *but Jessica must be right. Why else would Bruce act like such a jerk when I asked him a simple question? He's obviously got something to hide. And what he's hiding is the fact that he's only been hanging around with me until he wins that stupid election. And then I suppose he's just going to dump me—like all the others*, she thought bitterly. *I'm just like any other girl to him, and I was a fool to think that I really mattered.*

"Hey, what's wrong?" Bruce said suddenly. "Don't tell me *that's* what's been bothering you all afternoon."

Regina flinched. *He thinks I'm an idiot*, she thought furiously. *He thinks I can't figure out what's going on!* "Would you mind telling me once and for all what's going on with that election?" she demanded icily.

Bruce stared at her, his face a complete blank. "What in the world are you so angry about?" he demanded. "It has nothing to do with you!"

Regina burst into tears. *That's it*, she thought, fumbling with the clasp on her bracelet. *I can't believe I ever trusted him for a single minute*. "Bruce Patman," she sputtered, throwing the bracelet on the seat between them, "why don't you just take your expensive presents and your stupid promises and get out of here?"

"Wait a minute!" Bruce exploded. "What in the world is going on here? All I said—"

"And you can take your stupid necklace, too," Regina cried, unfastening the ruby pendant and hurling it at him. "Don't think I'm as helpless as I seem," she sobbed. "I'm wise to you, and so is everybody else!"

"I don't know what you're talking about," Bruce said angrily, his face darkening. "And apparently you don't want to tell me, either. You'd rather just throw things at me and tell me how horrible I've been. Regina, I don't think you're wise to anything. You've gone completely off the deep end. Can't you at least tell me what's—"

"If I've gone off the deep end," Regina said coldly, pulling the door handle with trembling fingers, "I won't force you to put up with my company for another minute. I never want to see you again as long as I live!" she shouted, pushing the door open and leaping out. She shot him an icy glare.

Bruce had been pushed too far to remain calm

any longer. "If that's what you want, that's what you're going to get," he said bitterly, turning the key in the ignition. "I can't believe I thought you were different," he added accusingly. "I thought you were really special. And now it turns out you're just as messed up as every other girl in this town!" He gunned the motor and drove around the circular driveway, tires squealing.

I'm sure he thought I was special, Regina thought angrily, tears streaming down her face. *Too special to figure out that he was only putting up with me so more people would vote for him in his stupid election. Well, I'm tired of being special. And I think it's time I did something so no one can ever accuse me of being "special" again.*

Dragging her feet, Regina walked up the flagstone path to the Morrows' front door. Now that Bruce was gone, there was no reason not to do the sensible thing and go ahead with Dr. Friederich's treatments.

And the sooner I go the better, Regina thought miserably. *Because the sooner I'm half a globe away from Sweet Valley, the sooner I'll forget Bruce.*

And under the circumstances, she told herself, forgetting Bruce Patman was the smartest thing she could possibly do.

"Are you sure Mrs. Morrow said to come over now?" Todd asked Elizabeth. "It doesn't look like anyone's at home."

Elizabeth looked at her watch. "She said five o'clock," she answered. "Oh, Todd, I'm afraid we'll never get this carnival together! Everything seems to be going wrong!"

"Don't worry," Todd said reassuringly. "We'll be all right. Things are bound to fall into place."

"I hope so," Elizabeth said anxiously, pressing the doorbell.

To her surprise, the door opened right away. An attractive, green-eyed boy grinned out at her, running his hand through his sandy hair. "You again!" he said, laughing. He opened the door wider to let Elizabeth and Todd come inside.

Elizabeth glanced at Todd and turned purposefully to the boy. "We've come to see Mrs. Morrow," she said firmly. "Are any of the Morrows here?"

"They've gone out for a little while. Emergency family business," he told her. Something about his expression made Elizabeth feel strange. *He looks as if he's seen me before*, she thought. *But I don't know who he is!*

"You haven't told me who your friend is," Donald added, staring past Elizabeth at Todd.

"My name is Todd," Todd told him, not sounding very happy.

"Donald Essex," the boy said, extending his hand. "I don't think we need to introduce ourselves, do we?" he said, turning back to Elizabeth. "You know, I've been thinking about your carnival, and it sounds pretty interesting. Do I still have an invitation for—when did you say it was?"

"I didn't," Elizabeth said, staring at him. What was going on here? she wondered. One thing was certain—Todd didn't like it very much. He was glowering the whole time that Donald Essex was speaking.

"That's right," Donald said, laughing. "You didn't. Well, when is it?" he asked. "I wouldn't mind helping out."

Elizabeth cleared her throat. "I think you must be making some kind of mistake," she began doubtfully.

Donald looked from Elizabeth to Todd and seemed to come to a quick conclusion. "Never mind," he said cheerfully. "I guess I *did* make a mistake," he added, winking at Elizabeth. "Can I take a message for Mrs. Morrow?"

"No, thanks," Elizabeth told him. "We'll call her later."

"What was that all about?" Todd demanded, following Elizabeth down the walk. "He seemed pretty friendly, Liz. Where'd you meet him?"

Elizabeth flushed. "I never met him before in my life."

"Sure didn't look that way, did it?" Todd asked mildly, opening the car door and sliding behind the driver's seat.

"Come on, Todd," Elizabeth said lightly,

getting into the car and fastening her seat belt. "I don't even *know* that guy!"

"Well, he sure seems to know *you*," Todd said moodily.

"I'm sure there's a perfectly logical—" Elizabeth began, but Todd cut her off midsentence.

"I'm sure there is, too," he said. "But right now I'd just prefer to drop the whole thing."

Elizabeth bit her lip. How had everything turned into such a mess all of a sudden? The carnival was only six days away, and Mrs. Morrow couldn't even keep an appointment to help plan it. Even worse, Todd was angry with her now.

This is going to be some week, Elizabeth thought, putting her head in her hands. *It hasn't even started yet, and already I wish it were over!*

Ten

Elizabeth turned the dial on her locker and rummaged grumpily through the books she kept stacked neatly inside. It was Monday morning, and the world looked considerably less cheerful than it had on Friday afternoon. "Something is wrong with my favorite twin," Jessica had said earlier that morning as she cheerfully buttered a piece of toast. Elizabeth hadn't even bothered to answer. She felt completely out of sorts, and Jessica's infamous grin didn't do much to lift her spirits.

For one thing, Elizabeth hadn't gotten much sleep the night before. She'd been up well past midnight trying to finalize plans for the carnival, and when she'd finally gotten into bed, all she could think about was the unhappy expression on Todd's face when he had dropped her off at home after their visit to the Morrows'.

He hadn't kissed her goodbye, and he hadn't called her later, the way he always did. Even worse, he wasn't waiting for her in the parking lot that morning. And she'd gotten to school early just to look for him.

"Liz," a voice said shyly at her shoulder now. "Can I talk to you for a few minutes? I was hoping I'd find you alone."

Elizabeth turned, and the frown faded from her face. "Of course, Regina," she said. "Why don't we go to the *Oracle* office and sit down?" she added on impulse. Something in Regina's expression suggested she wanted to have a long talk.

"It's nice in here," Regina commented several minutes later, looking around at the typewriters and piles of paper lining the small room.

Elizabeth giggled. "It's serviceable, anyway," she said, offering Regina a chair. "Jessica thinks it's absolutely hideous."

Regina looks different today, Elizabeth thought, sneaking a glance at her as she sat down. *She looks a lot older than she did when I saw her last. More serious—as if something big has happened.*

"Liz," Regina began, "I'm afraid I won't be able to be in the fashion show this Saturday after all. Don't worry," she added hastily, seeing the expression on Elizabeth's face. "My mother's going to come up with something to take its place. She feels bad enough as it is. Things have been so crazy around our house that she hasn't been much help to you."

"That's OK, Regina," Elizabeth assured her. "I'm just sorry you won't be able to do it. Is anything wrong?"

Regina flushed. "I'm leaving for Switzerland Friday morning," she said quietly. "My mother told me about the talk she had with you, Liz. I know you know all about the treatments. And I wanted to thank you for keeping quiet about it. It's important to me that no one find out before I go."

Elizabeth took Regina's hand, squeezing it warmly. "I'm so happy for you," she said, her voice breaking with emotion. "I'm going to miss you, Regina, but it'll be exciting when you come back!"

Regina sighed. "They're not one hundred percent certain that they can completely restore my hearing," she warned Elizabeth. "And I'll have to go through a lot of tests, but the way I see it, it's certainly worth a chance. I'm going to miss you, too, Liz," she added impulsively. "You've been such a wonderful friend."

Elizabeth fiddled with a piece of paper, her gaze turning thoughtful. "How does Bruce feel about your leaving?"

Regina flushed, tears welling up in her eyes. "He doesn't know," she said at last, looking away. "We haven't really spoken since I made up my mind."

"Is everything all right?" Elizabeth asked sympathetically.

Regina shook her head, tears spilling down her cheeks. "Oh, Liz," she gasped. "I've been such a fool!" Her voice choked with tears, Regina told Elizabeth the entire story, omitting only Jessica's role as informer.

"That's amazing," Elizabeth said when she had finished. "God, sometimes I could just kill Bruce Patman!"

"Do you think I'm really gullible?" Regina whispered, reaching for her handkerchief.

"No, I don't," Elizabeth said, giving her a hug. "But now that you've told me this, I'll admit I was never crazy about you and Bruce. You're far too good for him. And I think you're doing the right thing about Switzerland. The treatments may not be guaranteed, but you'd never forgive yourself if you didn't give them a chance."

"You're right, Liz," Regina said, wiping her eyes and smiling. "Thank you so much for everything."

Elizabeth sighed, closing the door to the *Oracle* office behind them as they left the room. *So*, she thought to herself, *I guess I was right about Bruce after all*.

But this was one time when Elizabeth would have preferred to be wrong.

"Hello, Elizabeth," Mr. Collins said cheerfully, looking up from his desk as she entered his room at lunchtime. "Is something keeping you from Sweet Valley High's *haute cuisine*, or did you come to talk business?"

Elizabeth laughed. "Both, I guess," she said slowly, sliding into a desk in the front row. Elizabeth didn't feel particularly hungry. Todd hadn't spoken to her all morning. It was obvious that he was trying to avoid her.

"How's the carnival coming?" Mr. Collins asked, putting his hands behind his head and leaning back in his chair.

"Fine, I think," Elizabeth told him. "We've had a few last-minute changes."

"Like Regina Morrow?" Mr. Collins asked.

"You know about that?" Elizabeth demanded, surprised.

Mr. Collins nodded. "I've got my fingers crossed for her," he said warmly. "It takes a lot of courage for her to uproot herself again now that she's finally settled in and made some real friends."

"And some *not* so real friends," Elizabeth mumbled.

Mr. Collins got up from his desk and walked over to the window, turning around to give

Elizabeth a penetrating look. "You don't think much of Bruce Patman, do you?" he asked.

Elizabeth shook her head. "I don't like the way he treats girls," she said.

Mr. Collins sat on the edge of his desk, swinging his legs. "Well, you're entitled to your opinion," he told her. "And if I know you, Liz, it's an opinion based on good judgment. But you know," he added slowly, "people *do* change. No one is all good or all bad. That only happens in old movies."

Elizabeth shook her head. "I'm sure you're right," she answered. "But I get so angry when I think of the way Bruce treated Regina!"

Mr. Collins laughed. "You're a good friend, that's why," he said. "And I don't blame you for being angry. But you may not have all the facts yet," he warned her.

Elizabeth's brow wrinkled. "But Regina said—"

"I know," Mr. Collins said, smiling. "But I also know how easy it is for two people to have a misunderstanding."

Like Todd and me, Elizabeth thought.

"All I'm saying," he added gently, "is to try to keep an open mind. It's what you're known for around here!" he teased.

Elizabeth burst out laughing. "I'll try my best, Mr. Collins," she promised. "I just hope you'll keep an open mind while I show you the final plans for the carnival!"

*   *   *

"Jessica," Elizabeth complained, "you're standing in my light. I've got to get this list to Mrs. Morrow as soon as I can."

"Do you realize," Jessica pointed out, "that you've turned into a real bore ever since this carnival business got started?"

The twins were out by the pool in the Wakefields' backyard, soaking up the last rays of afternoon sun. "Sorry, Jess," Elizabeth said dryly. "If you just let me get this finished, I promise I'll be my usual entertaining self."

Jessica flung herself down on a deck chair. "You sound pretty grumpy, Liz," she commented a moment later. "Are you sure the carnival's the only thing on your mind?"

"Absolutely," Elizabeth snapped. The last thing in the world she wanted to do was tell Jessica that Todd had been avoiding her. That would be one sure way of making it a bigger deal than it was already.

"My, aren't we touchy today," Jessica said indignantly, adjusting the strings on her new white bikini top.

"I thought you had to work on your term paper," Elizabeth said, staring at her twin, who was now lolling comfortably on the lounge chair with her eyes closed.

"Oh, yeah," Jessica said, opening one eye.

"You're right. I guess I'd better go to the library after dinner."

Elizabeth shook her head. "How you've made it through school this far is beyond me!"

"I do what I can," Jessica said sweetly.

Elizabeth frowned at the sheaf of papers in her hand. It wasn't any fun planning the carnival without Todd! She remembered what Mr. Collins had said to her during lunch and straightened her shoulders purposefully. *If Todd doesn't call tonight, I'm going to call him and straighten this whole mess out*, she vowed silently.

"By the way," Jessica murmured, both eyes closed, "you didn't see Bruce and Regina today, did you?"

"Not together," Elizabeth said, surprised. "I thought you'd know by now, Jess. You must be working too hard on that term paper of yours to keep up with local gossip," she added wryly.

"What gossip?" Jessica demanded, off the lounge chair and on her feet in a flash.

Elizabeth laughed. "That's the most life I've seen in you in weeks," she commented. "Bruce and Regina had a big fight," she added. "I don't think they'll be seeing much of each other anymore."

"Thank God," Jessica breathed, hugging herself delightedly.

Elizabeth looked at her twin strangely. "Breakups aren't usually a cause for celebration, are they?"

Jessica flushed. "I'm just relieved for Regina, that's all," she said defensively. "Bruce isn't good enough for her. She deserves someone really nice, and Bruce isn't."

Elizabeth laughed. "I must admit I agree with you there."

"What was their fight about?"

Elizabeth sighed. "You'll think it's really stupid."

"I won't," Jessica promised innocently.

"Well, Regina thinks Bruce was using her to get more votes for the presidency of the centennial committee. Probably not what you expected."

Jessica raised her eyebrows. "Not at all," she demurred. "Well, whatever the reason, I'm glad for Regina. Hey," she added suddenly, her blue-green eyes narrowing, "she didn't mention anything to you about Donald Essex, did she?"

"Donald who?" Elizabeth asked, turning back to her notes.

"Donald Essex," Jessica said dreamily. "You should see him, Liz. He's absolutely gorgeous—about six feet tall, sandy blond hair, and the most amazing eyes."

Elizabeth dropped her notebook, her eyes widening. "You didn't by any chance meet this male god at the Morrows', did you?"

Jessica nodded.

"And did you invite him to the carnival?" Elizabeth went on, her voice rising.

Jessica shrugged. "How was I supposed to know Regina liked him instead of Bruce?"

"She doesn't, you jerk!" Elizabeth cried, leaping to her feet. "I've got to make a phone call," she muttered, racing for the screen door.

Jessica shook her head and flipped her blond hair behind her shoulders. *Poor Liz*, she thought sadly. *She's really lost it. She's been racing around here like crazy ever since she took over this silly carnival.*

As for me, Jessica thought lazily, *I haven't a care in the world! And since it's a cinch I'm not going to the library tonight*, she added, a triumphant grin on her face, *maybe I should try to get in touch with Donald again*. She chuckled, rolled over on her stomach, and stretched contentedly in the sun.

Eleven

Jessica had rarely been in such fine spirits. Every time she passed Regina in the hall, she felt like hugging her. Jessica had dressed, on this first triumphant day of term paperlessness, in a brand-new pair of jeans and a tight white T-shirt. "Simple but effective," she told Elizabeth. Her generous mood extended to saying hello to Winston Egbert even before he accosted her in the cafeteria.

"Hi, Winston," she said merrily, twirling a silky blond strand of hair around her finger. "You haven't seen Lila anywhere, have you?"

"No," Winston said, "I haven't. But now that you're here, Jessica, may I include you in my random poll? Which would you find more satisfying to hurl at my face—whipped-cream pie or lemon?"

"Whipped cream," Jessica told him. "Are you sure you haven't seen her? We were supposed to meet here five minutes ago."

"She may have slipped past me somehow," Winston admitted. "I've been busy tallying up the results of my poll. So far we have fifty-seven votes for whipped cream and only fourteen for lemon."

"There she is!" Jessica exclaimed, spotting Lila on the patio adjoining the cafeteria. "Good luck, Winston. I've got to go now."

"Thanks!" Winston called as Jessica hurried away.

"I've been looking for you everywhere," Jessica complained, hurling herself dramatically onto the bench across from Lila.

"I'll bet you have," Lila said grumpily.

"Cheer up," Jessica crooned. "A term paper or two will take your mind off it."

Lila frowned. "You shouldn't gloat, Jessica. It's vulgar."

Jessica giggled. "Don't be a poor loser, Lila. Admit it. I've won, fair and square. And you owe me one complete term paper, fifteen pages long—signed, sealed, and delivered by the end of next week."

"OK, OK," Lila said mildly. "I get the idea."

"So," Jessica said, a smile playing about her

lips, "are you going to the library after school today?"

Lila shrugged. "I don't know," she replied. "I was planning to stop by my father's building and see if that guy Jack is around."

"Lila! You've only got a week and a half to write two entire term papers!" Jessica shrieked.

Lila yawned, making a show of covering her mouth with her hand. "Don't be so dramatic," she said languidly. "Things get done if you don't panic, Jess. Worrying about them is useless."

Jessica stared in amazement, her high spirits suddenly dampened. It had just occurred to her that winning this bet wasn't necessarily the end of her troubles. "You'll do a good job on it, won't you?" she asked anxiously. "I really need to pull my history grade up."

"Take it easy, Jess!" Lila said, laughing. "You don't have to panic!"

Yes I do, Jessica thought, gripping the table with both hands. *If Lila doesn't get me a good grade on this paper, I'm as good as dead!*

"The best thing about arguing with you," Todd murmured, kissing Elizabeth's ear softly, "is making up again." It was lunchtime, and they were sitting under one of the oak trees on the lawn of the school.

"This was the stupidest fight we've ever had." Elizabeth laughed. "I can't believe it didn't occur to either of us that Donald thought I was Jessica."

"Poor Donald." Todd grinned and shook his head. "First your sister turns up and flirts with him like crazy. And then you turn up with me and give him the cold shoulder."

Elizabeth giggled. "I'd never seen him before," she said. "And suddenly he wanted to come to the carnival with me! Jess sure moves fast," she added admiringly.

"Well, we acted like a pair of idiots, that's for sure," Todd told her. "I can't believe we wasted a whole day feeling awful over such a stupid misunderstanding."

"And I can't believe I didn't think of Jessica the minute the whole thing came up—especially since I knew she'd been over at the Morrows' talking to Regina about the carnival," Elizabeth said.

"You've had a lot on your mind," Todd reminded her. "I think all this carnival business is wearing you out."

Elizabeth nodded, leaning against him with a sigh. "You're probably right," she said softly.

"There isn't anything else bothering you, is there?" Todd continued. "You do seem sort of preoccupied lately."

Elizabeth was quiet for a moment. "Well, I *have* been thinking about Regina," she admitted. "I know it's none of my business, Todd, but

Bruce makes me furious! Regina is incredibly vulnerable, and she really trusted him. And then she finds out that he's just been using her all along. I think it's horrible."

Todd's brow wrinkled. "It's a strange story," he said quietly. "Liz, I know you don't like Bruce, and I know you have good reason to feel the way you do. But I'm not sure I'm completely convinced that he was using Regina."

"What do you mean?" Elizabeth asked. "It sure sounds like he was."

"It's just a hunch," Todd told her. "And I may be wrong. But I've been watching Bruce the last couple of days, and he looks miserable to me. In fact, he looks like he's lost his best friend."

Elizabeth smiled. "You just think everyone's as sensitive as you are," she said, giving his shoulder a quick kiss.

"Hey," Todd said suddenly, lowering his voice. "Don't look now, but the Beast is coming toward us. And it looks as if he's got something serious on his mind."

Elizabeth turned her head. Sure enough, Bruce Patman was walking slowly toward them, his hands in his pockets and his head lowered.

"Sorry to bother you two," Bruce said, sitting down on the grass near them.

Todd's right, Elizabeth thought, taking a good look at Bruce. *He looks as if he hasn't slept in days. But that doesn't mean he really misses Regina*, she reminded herself. *He's probably just angry because his little plan got fouled up. Now no one will vote for him, and he'll lose his precious election.*

"What can we do for you, Bruce?" Todd asked cheerfully, his arm still around Elizabeth's shoulder.

"Well, actually," Bruce mumbled, a hint of red coming to his face, "it was Liz I really wanted to talk to. Do you think you might be able to come by the house later this afternoon?" he asked Elizabeth.

Elizabeth stared at him, her eyes narrowing. "Why?" she asked, trying to ignore the slight pressure of Todd's hand on her shoulder. *I don't care what Todd says*, she thought stubbornly. *As far as I'm concerned, Bruce Patman is a snake. And I don't want anything to do with him.*

"Liz, I need your advice," Bruce said, leaning forward in his chair. "I know how much Regina admires you, and I know she tells you things, too. It's not easy for me to ask for help," Bruce added, "but I'm asking now. I need to talk to you, Liz. Will you come by?"

"I'll come," Elizabeth said simply. Todd patted her arm approvingly, but Elizabeth didn't respond. *But I'm not happy about it*, she added silently. *And as far as I'm concerned, Regina is lucky to be rid of you!*

"You sure I can't get you something to drink?"

Bruce asked, drumming his fingers nervously on the table.

Elizabeth shook her head. "I can't stay long. The carnival is this Saturday, and we've still got a lot of work to do."

Elizabeth and Bruce were out on the patio overlooking the Patmans' Olympic-sized swimming pool. Late afternoon sunlight poured through the trees, glinting on the water's surface. It was a beautiful day and a beautiful setting, but Elizabeth couldn't wait to leave. She felt uncomfortable around Bruce, and the tense, distracted look on his face wasn't making her feel any more at ease.

"Liz, I'll be honest with you," Bruce said abruptly, running a hand through his hair. "I know how you feel about me, and I don't blame you. I've done some pretty obnoxious things. When things haven't gone right for me, I guess I always knew that I deserved what I got—and sometimes worse. But Regina—" He broke off, his voice choked with emotion.

"Bruce, I really don't feel comfortable talking about this," Elizabeth said quickly, getting to her feet and reaching for her purse. "I'm sorry about you and Regina, but it doesn't have anything to do with me. So I'll just get going now, and—"

"Liz, please!" Bruce interrupted, his eyes shining with tears. "Listen to me," he said desperately. "You're one of Regina's closest friends. Did she say anything to you about why she broke up with me? Did she give you any clue, any little hint? I've been up night after night trying to figure it out. I've gone back over every conversation we had, racking my brain, trying to guess what could have made her hate me. And I come up with"—he shook his head, staring pleadingly at Elizabeth—"nothing. Absolutely nothing."

Elizabeth sat back down, her eyes troubled. "You mean you really don't know?" she asked him, puzzled.

Bruce put his hands up in a gesture of despair. "Do you think I'd drag you over here and beg you like this if I knew?" he asked.

Elizabeth took a deep breath. Maybe Todd was right. What she saw before her wasn't the Bruce Patman she'd known and hated at all. He really *did* look miserable. What's more, he looked as though he was telling the truth. "Why didn't you tell Regina you were running for president of the centennial committee?" Elizabeth asked him.

Bruce stared at her. "What are you talking about?" he cried. "What does that have to do with anything?"

Elizabeth sighed. "Regina thought you kept it from her on purpose. She thinks you started seeing her to make yourself more popular so you could win the election."

Bruce looked dumbfounded. "You're kidding," he said, staring at Elizabeth as if she'd just gone mad.

Elizabeth shook her head. "She thought that was why you kept the election quiet. Because you were using her so you could win."

Bruce shook his head. "I can't believe it," he said quietly. "Liz, I signed up for that election last Thursday. That was five days ago! And I've known Regina for weeks! The reason I didn't mention that I was running was that I was going to surprise her if I won. It was just something I wanted to do at the last minute. Because I was so happy to live in Sweet Valley after I met Regina," he added softly. "I wanted to give something back to the town."

Elizabeth bit her lip. "You're telling the truth now, aren't you?" she asked quietly.

Bruce stared at her. "Liz, for the first time in my life, I had something that I really cared for. Maybe you think people are the way they are, and that's it. Well, it doesn't happen to have been true in my case. When you fall in love with someone, you change. And when you fall in love with someone like Regina, you change for the better—fast. I'm sure there's a lot of apologizing I ought to do now for the way I used to behave. But right now, Liz, I don't feel like doing anything before I apologize to Regina. I've just got to make her understand!"

"Bruce, wait a minute," Elizabeth said, putting her hand on his arm. "I'm sorry I doubted you," she added. "I was wrong. But there's something I have to tell you before you try to find Regina."

"What is it?" Bruce asked, his eyes fixed attentively on hers.

Elizabeth looked down at the table. "Regina is supposed to leave for Switzerland," she told him. "And if you explain what happened to her, she may not go."

"Switzerland!" Bruce cried, his eyes flashing with horror. "That's all the more reason to find her right away, then!" He jumped up from the table, his hands trembling.

"Bruce, wait a minute!" Elizabeth insisted. "She's going there to undergo treatments that may restore her hearing. She didn't tell you about it because she refused to leave you. And if you go find her now, she'll never go."

Bruce sank back into his chair, his face drained of color. "How long have you known about this?" he demanded.

"Not very long," Elizabeth said softly. "Regina's mother told me last week. She begged me to help change Regina's mind, but I was afraid to interfere."

When Bruce looked up again, his eyes were

soft and moist. "You mean Regina might be able to hear again—*really* hear?" he asked her.

Elizabeth nodded. "The treatments aren't guaranteed, but the doctor thinks Regina is a good candidate."

"That's wonderful!" Bruce cried. "She can go to Switzerland, have the treatments, and when she comes back, we'll have the whole summer together!"

Elizabeth sighed. "These are pretty complicated operations, Bruce. It's not just a matter of a couple of weeks."

"What are you saying, Liz?" Bruce demanded. "How long will she have to be away?"

"A long time," Elizabeth told him. "Mrs. Morrow told me it could be a year."

Bruce didn't say a word. He got up from the table and walked across the patio, where he stared out over Sweet Valley. "The poor kid," he said at last, still not looking at Elizabeth. "And she never said a word about it."

"Bruce, what are you going to do?" Elizabeth asked anxiously. Bruce couldn't go to Regina now! It would ruin everything. Regina would never leave him, and she'd never hear again.

"I don't know," Bruce said softly, turning back to face her with a look of helplessness that made her wince. "I just don't know, Liz. If I let her go now, thinking that I never loved her—" He

116

broke off, turning away again, but not before Elizabeth saw his face.

I never would have believed it in a million years, she thought. *Bruce Patman is crying.*

Twelve

It was after midnight, but Bruce couldn't sleep. The things Elizabeth had told him earlier that afternoon kept coming back to him, mixed with the words Regina had shouted at him when they had parted. Lying on his four-poster bed with his hands behind his head, Bruce stared into the darkness, trying to decide what to do.

He wanted Regina to be with him forever. The thought of an entire year without her filled him with dread. How could he let her leave him? He couldn't, he thought to himself. He just couldn't.

Turning the lamp on beside his bed, Bruce got up and wandered over to his desk. He opened the top drawer, rummaging through the papers inside until he found what he was looking for. It was a photograph of Regina he had taken weeks ago at the beach. Her head was thrown back in the picture, her eyes were lit up with excitement, her black hair gleamed against her cream-white skin. "She's so beautiful," he said softly, putting the picture down.

For a long time he sat at his desk, holding his chin in his hand and staring down at Regina's image. He could hear the grandfather clock downstairs chiming the hour. It was one o'clock, and still he was as alert as if it were the middle of the day. Then, picking up a pen and taking a clean sheet of paper from his desk drawer, he began to write.

It seemed as though no time had passed at all before he heard the clock strike two o'clock. He leaned back, holding the sheet of paper before him, and began to read.

Dear Regina,
By the time you read this, it will be too late for you to change your mind about the treatments. And you mustn't change your mind, my dearest—not for anything. Elizabeth told me everything, and I must admit that at first all I could think of was rushing over to your house and putting things right again.

I never cared about anything but you. I signed up to run in the election last Thursday—exactly five days ago.

I was wrong not to mention it to you at once, but I wanted to surprise you if I won. I can't believe you could ever imagine my using you. I love you with all my heart, and always will.

In fact it's because I love you that I can't explain all this to you before Friday. If there's the slightest chance that you might be able to hear again one day after these treatments, you must go through with them.

I'm not selfish enough to let you stay in Sweet Valley for my sake, Regina. But I'm too selfish to let you go thinking badly of me. You must know that I've loved you with all my heart from the first.

It's not perfect, Bruce thought, *but it's how I feel.* With a great sigh, he picked his pen up again and signed his name at the bottom of the page. When the clock chimed again, Bruce was still sitting at his desk. He had a feeling it was going to be a long time before he got a peaceful night's sleep.

"Come on, you guys," Elizabeth said. "Today's Wednesday. We've got exactly three days left to pull this carnival together, and about three months of work left to do."

The committee was meeting in Mr. Collins's

room, and Elizabeth was doing her best to channel the group's high spirits.

"The prizes and decorations are all ready," Olivia told her, lifting a stuffed animal out of an enormous box.

"Actually, we're in pretty good shape as far as games go," Todd told Elizabeth, giving her a sympathetic smile across the room. Mr. Collins was almost half an hour late, and Elizabeth was getting worried.

"OK," Elizabeth said, making check marks in her notebook. "Prizes are ready. Games are ready. Ken, how do the booths look?"

"We've been setting them up today in the football field," Ken told her. "We've got one tent up already, and about half of the booths are ready."

"Good," Elizabeth said, looking relieved. "Winston, are you ready to be the master of ceremonies?"

"Never readier," Winston assured her. "I'm going to borrow a portable microphone from the office so people can hear me better."

"OK," Elizabeth said, ignoring the groans from around the room.

"Olivia, would you mind helping me at the ticket booth? Tickets will be a dollar each, and a ticket entitles you to play a game at any booth."

"Sure," Olivia said agreeably, bursting into laughter as she saw Winston throw his arms

121

around a large stuffed rabbit and give it a passionate kiss.

"Hi, everyone!" Mr. Collins boomed, opening the door a crack and sticking his head inside. "Am I too late, or may I still come in?"

"Come in, come in!" Winston boomed, using the rabbit as a microphone. Elizabeth looked up in surprise. Mr. Collins wasn't alone, and he seemed unusually flustered as he strolled over to his desk.

"Mind if I sit in on this meeting?" Nora Dalton asked, following Mr. Collins into the room and sliding into an empty desk in the front of the room.

"You may have to buy a ticket." Olivia giggled.

Elizabeth caught Ms. Dalton's eye and smiled. She had always liked the pretty young French teacher, and she was happy to see her now. At twenty-five, black-haired, bright-eyed Ms. Dalton was the youngest member of Sweet Valley High's staff. Her bubbly personality made her a favorite with most of her students.

"We were just getting to the refreshment stands," Enid explained to Mr. Collins. "Caroline promised to make some of her disgustingly rich brownies, and Todd and I are making pizza. Does anyone else have any suggestions?"

"There's always rabbit," Winston pointed out, waving the stuffed rabbit in the air. Everyone laughed, and in the pause that followed, Nora Dalton spoke up.

"We could have an international food stand," she suggested. "If you want, Enid, I could help with it. I can make crepes."

"As long as we don't have to order in French," Todd said, grinning.

"That's a wonderful idea," Elizabeth said. "Well," she added, flipping quickly through her notebook, "it looks as though we're in pretty good shape. Mr. Collins, would you mind if I went out to the football field with Todd and Ken to see how the booths look?"

"Go right ahead," Mr. Collins told her. "I'll stay here and see how many exotic international dishes I can coax out of these chefs."

"That was kind of a surprise, don't you think?" Todd asked, putting his arm around Elizabeth as they headed outside to the field.

"You mean Mr. Collins and Ms. Dalton? It's not the first time I've seen them together," Ken said, winking at Todd.

Elizabeth flushed. She liked Mr. Collins too much to feel comfortable hearing gossip about him. "I'm sure it's no big deal," she said lightly, quickening her step.

"Liz is probably right," Todd said quickly, sensing her annoyance. "And anyway, what they do is their business. Right, Liz?"

Elizabeth was about to agree with him when she heard someone shouting her name behind them.

"Hey, it's Bruce," Todd told her, turning around and shading his eyes with his hand. "And it looks like he's trying to win the Bart again or something, he's running out here so fast."

"These days he's trying to win everything," Ken pointed out, looking annoyed.

Elizabeth followed Todd's gaze. "I'll tell you what," she said quickly. "Why don't you two go ahead, and I'll catch up with you. This looks kind of urgent."

"OK," Todd agreed, kissing her on the cheek. "But don't be too long. We need your professional opinion on our expert carpentry."

Todd and Ken went on ahead, and Elizabeth turned around to wait for Bruce. She didn't have long to wait. Bruce crossed the field a minute later, breathing heavily as he slowed down before her.

"Liz!" he gasped, wiping his forehead with his hand. "I'm glad I caught you."

Elizabeth giggled. "It would have been impossible to miss me at that pace," she told him. Her expression changed when she saw how serious he looked. "Are you all right?" she asked soberly. "I thought about calling you, but I didn't think I should butt in any further than I have already."

Bruce shook his head. "No, Liz, you were right to tell me what you did. I thought about calling you, too, but to be honest I haven't really felt like talking very much."

"I understand," Elizabeth said sympathetically. "What's that?" she asked curiously, noticing a white envelope in Bruce's right hand.

"It's a letter for Regina," Bruce told her. "That's why I came chasing after you, Liz. I was afraid I wouldn't be able to find you later, and I need to ask you a favor."

Elizabeth's heart quickened. What did the letter say? Had Bruce decided not to confront Regina and explain what had really happened? It seemed too much to hope for. Elizabeth had been thinking of little else since her talk with Bruce the day before. And all day she'd been afraid to run into Regina—afraid that Regina would say she had changed her mind about Switzerland.

"The letter explains what really happened with the election," Bruce said quietly. "Liz, I just couldn't bear to have Regina believe that I used her. I love her too much for that."

"I see," Elizabeth said quietly. *But if you* really *loved her*, she thought angrily, *you wouldn't explain a thing. That way she could still go to*

Switzerland—and maybe, just maybe, regain her hearing.

"The reason I need your help," Bruce continued, "is that I don't want Regina to read the letter until she's in Switzerland. And the only idea I can come up with is for you to sneak it into her suitcase—deep down where she won't find it for a while—sometime before she goes Friday morning. Liz, will you do that for me?"

Elizabeth stared at him. At first she wasn't sure she'd heard him correctly. "You mean you want Regina to go to Switzerland?" she asked doubtfully.

"Of course I don't," Bruce said fiercely. "I want her to stay right here. I've never wanted anything so badly in my whole life."

"Then why wait?" Elizabeth asked. "Why not take the letter to her now?"

"Because," Bruce said painfully, "I love her. And I want what's best for her. If there's a chance she can be cured, Regina owes it to herself to give it a try."

Elizabeth looked at Bruce wonderingly. *Mr. Collins was right*, she thought. *People* can *change.*

"I never could have imagined your making this kind of sacrifice before, Bruce," she said softly. On an impulse, she leaned forward and kissed him on the cheek.

"I never could have done it before," Bruce

said, clearing his throat. "You can't make a sacrifice until you love someone."

Elizabeth stared at him, resolve flashing in her blue-green eyes. "Give me the letter, Bruce," she said firmly. "I'll make sure it gets in Regina's suitcase."

Thirteen

"Elizabeth!" Mrs. Morrow exclaimed, opening the front door and smiling. "Come in, dear. Regina's upstairs getting her things together."

"I'm so glad I made it here before you left for the airport," Elizabeth said, stepping into the foyer. "I was afraid you'd leave before I had a chance to say goodbye to Regina."

Mrs. Morrow looked at her watch. "We've still got twenty minutes," she told her. Elizabeth couldn't get over the change in Mrs. Morrow. Her dark hair was swept back from her face in a neat ponytail, and her eyes were glowing with excitement. She looked carefree and happy as a girl.

"Was that someone at the door, Mom?"

Regina asked, bounding down the stairs. "I thought I saw a car coming up the drive." Catching sight of Elizabeth, Regina's lovely face clouded over briefly, then she smiled. "Liz!" she exclaimed. "It's you!"

I wonder if she was still hoping Bruce would come, Elizabeth thought sympathetically. She reached inside her book bag and brushed Bruce's letter with her fingertips. It was still there. Suddenly Elizabeth was filled with a rush of warmth and admiration for Bruce. How much easier it would have been for him to come over here, take Regina in his arms, and explain what had happened! And how incredibly hard it must be for him to stay away, knowing that within a few hours Regina would be on a plane, out of reach of his apologies!

"Will you come upstairs?" Regina was asking her. "I've still got a few things to pack, and Mom'll kill me if I'm late."

Mrs. Morrow gave her daughter a warm hug. "I couldn't care less how long it takes you," she said, her voice thick with emotion. "Go on!" She pushed Regina playfully toward the stairs. "And don't forget your passport," she reminded her.

Upstairs Elizabeth sank down on the flowered bedspread covering Regina's double bed. Watching her friend hurrying from her dresser to the open suitcase near her door, Elizabeth felt a lump come into her throat. "I'm going to miss you, Regina," she said softly.

Regina smiled at her, her blue eyes surprisingly calm. "I'm going to miss you, too," she said firmly, taking a scrapbook out of her top drawer and flipping through it. "It's funny," she added, "I don't think I've ever been as happy as I've been since I came to Sweet Valley."

"Can I see some of your snapshots?" Elizabeth asked. Regina nodded and handed her the book. "Are you taking this with you?" Elizabeth continued, reaching inside her book bag for Bruce's letter.

Regina disappeared into her closet. "I don't know," she said sadly. "It's silly to try to hang on to the past, Liz. What matters is the future."

Elizabeth tucked Bruce's letter inside the scrapbook, next to a picture of Bruce and Regina at the beach. She waited until Regina came out of the closet to answer.

"Nonsense," she told her, handing her the scrapbook. "This isn't the past, Regina. The people in this book aren't going to forget you while you're away. And I don't think you should forget them, either."

For the second time that morning, Regina's face clouded over. For a minute, Elizabeth was afraid Regina was going to break down and cry. Then, pulling her long hair back from her face and giving Elizabeth a radiant smile, she took the scrapbook and fit it into a large canvas shoulder bag next to her suitcase.

"You're right, Liz," Regina said. "I don't want to forget anything that's happened this year. Not even the bad parts," she added softly.

Elizabeth threw her arms around her and gave her a big hug. "Please keep in touch," she begged. "And I want you to know that we're all behind you. *All* of us," she added firmly.

It would be a long time, Elizabeth thought to herself, before she forgot the expression on Regina's face as she stood in the front doorway to the Morrows' estate, sadly waving goodbye.

"Where've you been?" Todd asked Elizabeth anxiously, jumping up to pull a chair out for her at the crowded lunch table. The carnival would be held the next day, and the committee had arranged one last meeting to make sure everything was in order.

"At Regina's," Elizabeth told him quietly. "She's leaving for Switzerland today, and I wanted to say goodbye." Todd didn't know yet that Elizabeth had promised Bruce to hide his letter in Regina's suitcase, but she figured there'd be time enough to tell him about it later.

Now there was something else Elizabeth was worried about. "Has anybody voted for centennial president yet?" she asked casually, looking around the table.

"I never vote in the morning," Winston said solemnly. "I prefer to deliberate all day and then reach my decision."

Olivia laughed. "I wish I had the same excuse," she said merrily, holding Roger's hand tightly in her own. "I haven't voted yet, either. But it's not because I want to deliberate. I just haven't had the time this morning."

"Neither have I," Roger said, grinning at Olivia.

"Pretty incriminating," Winston observed, and everyone laughed.

"Why do you ask, Liz?" Olivia inquired.

"I don't know," she said slowly. "I guess I'm just thinking out loud."

"When *I* think out loud, you can't hear a thing." Winston laughed.

"Winston!" Olivia exclaimed. "Give Elizabeth a chance to say what's on her mind."

"It's just this," Elizabeth added slowly. "I feel ashamed of the way I've talked about Bruce the last few weeks. I think I've really misjudged him."

"What do you mean?" Roger asked, leaning forward.

"I guess I just assumed that people are the way they are and can't change," Elizabeth admitted. "And that doesn't seem to be true in Bruce's case at all." Then, taking a deep breath, Elizabeth proceeded to tell the group the entire story, starting with the misunderstanding between Bruce and Regina and ending with Bruce's decision not to confront Regina, but to apologize instead in a letter so she wouldn't change her mind about Switzerland. "I'd never have expected Bruce to make this kind of sacrifice," Elizabeth concluded. "And, to be honest, I feel terrible for having been so skeptical of his affection for Regina. I know now that he really does love her. And the qualities he's exhibited these last few days have convinced me that he'd be the finest representative our school could possibly send to the centennial committee."

"That's the saddest story I've ever heard," Olivia whispered. "Do you think they'll ever see each other again?"

"I hope so," Elizabeth said. "They certainly deserve to have things work out."

"And Regina left this morning believing Bruce had used her?" Roger said, shaking his head. "Poor guy," he added. "That poor, poor guy. So that's why he's been acting so miserable this whole week!"

"What about Regina?" Olivia asked. "Can you imagine what must be going through her head right now? All by herself, having left her friends and family, going to a country where she doesn't even speak the language . . . and all the while not even knowing that Bruce still loves her?"

"One thing's for sure," Winston declared, his

cheerful face suddenly serious. "Bruce Patman *has* changed for the better. And I think Liz is absolutely right. He deserves to win this election!"

"Hear, hear!" Roger yelled. "Thank heavens we *didn't* vote this morning," he said to Olivia. "It just goes to show that tardiness has its virtues."

"My sentiments exactly," Winston agreed, taking a big bite of his sandwich.

Elizabeth looked around the table, a big smile on her face. She realized she felt much better about Bruce. And what had made her feel better was admitting that she was wrong. Mr. Collins had known what he was talking about, she thought happily, giving Todd's hand a warm squeeze under the table. People really could change, and it had been terrible of her not to give Bruce a chance.

I just hope, she thought anxiously, *that Regina's willing to give him a chance when she finds that letter.*

"Ladies and gentlemen," the stewardess announced, "Captain Rolfe has turned off the seat-belt sign. Please feel free to move about the cabin if you choose. And just sit back and enjoy the rest of your flight!"

Regina looked listlessly at the magazine in her lap. She wished she could be more excited about meeting Dr. Friederich and beginning her treatments. But deep inside Regina didn't feel excited about anything anymore.

The day she and Bruce had had their big fight, Regina felt as if a light had gone out inside her. Since then, she hadn't felt any joy about events taking place around her. She felt as though she were watching things from a great distance or as though they were happening to someone else— like a girl in a book.

Her parents had been so thrilled when she announced her decision to go to Switzerland. And at first Regina had gotten caught up in their excitement as they told her about the family Dr. Friederich had arranged for her to stay with. But for the last few days she had felt entirely numb. She had moved like a ghost from room to room in the Morrows' house, looking absently at the places where she had loved to sit and read or lie in the sun. At the back of her mind one question kept coming back to her again and again, like a refrain: would Bruce come see her before she left? He wouldn't let her go without saying goodbye! He just couldn't!

That morning, when she had seen Elizabeth's car in the driveway, a last rush of hope had flooded over her. Maybe Bruce's Porsche had broken down. Maybe he had borrowed a red Fiat from someone. Maybe he'd come at last to say goodbye, to hold her in his arms.

But it hadn't been Bruce after all. It had been

Elizabeth, and fond as she was of Elizabeth, Regina had felt almost crushed with disappointment. *I hope it didn't show in my face*, she thought. *Liz has been such a good friend to me. She was so right to insist that I bring my scrapbook—I'd be lost without it.*

Thinking of the scrapbook now, Regina felt mixed emotions. She wanted so badly to look at all the pictures she'd collected in her short time at Sweet Valley. But she knew that Bruce's pictures would be there among them. How would it feel to look down at his face, knowing she might never see him again?

With a sigh, Regina pulled the scrapbook from the bag she had stowed beneath the seat in front of her. *I don't care*, she told herself. *Bruce is part of the past, and the sooner I realize that, the better.* Flipping the album open, she saw the envelope Elizabeth had slipped inside. Curious, she took the letter from the envelope and began to read.

Anyone watching Regina as she read Bruce's letter would have seen a remarkable change in the girl's expression. At first her face turned bright red, then terribly pale, and then red again. Her lovely blue eyes, which had expressed a false serenity for the last week, filled with tears. "What a fool I've been," she said at last, laying the precious letter on her lap.

But the tears that finally flooded down Regina's cheeks had nothing to do with herself. She was thinking only of Bruce and the pain and loneliness he must have suffered. *And I thought it was hard for me*, she thought. *The whole time he was in anguish, too.*

It was hard for Regina to believe now that she had ever distrusted Bruce. *I don't know what got into me*, she thought, impatiently brushing away her tears.

Despite her remorse, Regina felt a sudden and overwhelming sensation of joy. *He still loves me*, she thought in wonder. *Enough to sit by in silence and let me go ahead with my decision. Enough to sacrifice his own happiness for my welfare.*

Regina believed now that she really had made the right decision. If Bruce, who loved her more than anyone, was willing to remain quiet so that she would go, she must have done the right thing.

"What's this?" Regina said aloud, feeling a tiny lump in the envelope. She withdrew the fine gold chain with the ruby pendant. *Elizabeth was right*, she thought, a lump in her throat. *My love for Bruce isn't part of the past. It's only just beginning.*

With a smile breaking over her face despite her tears, Regina fastened the ruby pendant around her neck. It was there, she told herself, for keeps.

Fourteen

Saturday, the day of the carnival, proved to be another beautiful day. Elizabeth, Todd, and Ken had been working all morning in the tents set up on the football field, and their efforts showed in the final results. The banners Olivia had designed snapped gaily in the breeze over the two yellow- and white-striped tents. Inside, one tent was filled with games—a ring toss, bowling pins, a wheel of fortune, as well as various booths designed by students. The other tent, much smaller than the first, was filled with refreshments.

By one o'clock the carnival was in full swing. Ms. Dalton and Enid were running the refreshment stands, serving everything from exotic French crepes to all-American brownies.

Winston Egbert, looking particularly lanky in his father's oversized tuxedo and red suspenders, was booming into a microphone before the large tent.

"Step right up, ladies and gentlemen! Welcome to the first ever Fowler Memorial Hospital/Sweet Valley High fund-raising carnival! Tickets are on sale right at the door, ladies and gentlemen, right at the door! For just one dollar—for one dollar only—you can take your chances in one of our challenging booths. Or you can take your chances at the refreshment stand. As you choose!"

"Don't you think he's going to drive everyone crazy in about an hour?" Jessica said grumpily, coming up behind Elizabeth and Todd.

"Jess! I've been looking for you everywhere," Elizabeth said happily. She couldn't believe how well everything was working out. The carnival seemed to be a roaring success. The field was crowded with familiar faces, both from school and from the community. "Look, there's Mrs. Patman," Elizabeth said to Todd, looking over at the small tent, where Marie Patman was presiding over a group of her friends. "Haven't the children done a *lovely* job?" she was saying loudly. "Of course you know that Henry and I are matching whatever money they raise today. It's the very *least* we can do for such a worthwhile cause."

"I wonder where Bruce is," Elizabeth mused. "Jess, you haven't seen Bruce anywhere, have you?"

Jessica grimaced. "No," she said sourly, "I haven't. And with luck I can keep things that way."

"What's eating her?" Todd asked, watching Jessica walk away.

"I don't know." Elizabeth sighed. "It's hard to keep up with her these days. I'm sure it's nothing very important."

"Hey," Todd said suddenly, starting to laugh, "Winston's setting up his booth. Let's go take a look, Liz."

Sure enough, Winston was transporting himself, microphone and all, into the large tent. Once inside he put his head through a hole in a board, and cajoled the crowd to throw pies at him.

"A dollar a throw! A dollar a throw! It's the bargain of the century, ladies and gentlemen. For merely one hundred copper pennies you have the satisfaction of hurling a large, fresh whipped-cream pie at my face! Step right up, ladies and gentlemen!"

Elizabeth burst out laughing as Mr. Collins stepped up to throw the first pie. Taking careful aim, he hurtled the pie, hitting Winston square in the face. For a minute the class clown looked completely dumbfounded as he reached out from behind the board to wipe the cream from his eyes. But the next minute he was laughing as hard as the crowd that had gathered to watch him. "Leave it to Winston." Todd grinned. "He even looks happy with pie all over him."

Later, Elizabeth and Todd were at the refreshment stand with Enid when Winston made a surprise announcement. "Ladies and gentlemen," his voice boomed. "We have a special speech this afternoon from our parent adviser for the carnival, Mrs. Skye Morrow. If you could all file into the large tent in ten minutes, you'll be able to hear what she has to say."

"Did you know about this?" Enid asked, looking puzzled.

Elizabeth shook her head. "Not at all," she replied, obviously surprised. "She did say something about finding a way to replace the mother-daughter fashion show, but with Regina leaving and all, I thought she forgot."

"Let's go," Todd said eagerly. "I want to hear this."

Several minutes later, the big tent was filled with attentive faces. All the game booths were left vacant as Mrs. Morrow climbed up on a small platform at the rear of the tent. Winston passed her his microphone, and she coughed nervously into it, caught the reassuring glances of Nicholas and her husband, and smiled.

For the first time, Elizabeth was able to envision Mrs. Morrow as she must have been in her youth. Wearing a simple green silk dress and a pair of low-heeled pumps, she looked so beautiful and poised it was hard for Elizabeth not to stare. Mrs. Morrow's black hair was brushed back from her face, and her high cheekbones and luminous eyes reminded Elizabeth of Regina. Looking around the tent for Bruce, she wondered if he saw the resemblance, too.

"The story I've chosen to tell you today is a true one," Mrs. Morrow said, her voice clear and strong. "It's about a little girl with a handicap and what she was able to do to overcome that handicap and live a normal life."

In the same rich, confident voice, Mrs. Morrow went on to tell the audience about Regina. She didn't seem to have prepared a speech, because her words were so natural and spontaneous. She told the audience about Regina's defect at birth and the difficulties she faced while she was growing up. Then Mrs. Morrow described the things Regina had been able to learn with the help of special schools and teachers. Finally, she told the audience about Dr. Friederich and his treatments in Switzerland. "We don't know yet what will happen to Regina," she concluded. "But what we do know is that children like her need help. Regina was very lucky to have a family who had the means to get all the help for her she needed. The children at Fowler Memorial Hospital aren't all so lucky. With your help we can overcome their handicaps and give them the opportunities that so many of us take for granted."

A hushed silence followed this speech. Elizabeth had never seen her classmates so moved. After a moment or two, scattered applause broke out across the tent, until everyone was clapping as loudly as possible. Mrs. Morrow raised her hand. "Just one more thing," she said into the microphone. "I'm afraid my own child has kept me so busy this week that I haven't been able to help the children at the hospital. In fact, I've been a very neglectful adviser," she admitted. "I'd just like to take this moment to thank Elizabeth Wakefield, who has done a phenomenal job of bringing all of us together today."

To her surprise and embarrassed pleasure, the whole tent went wild with applause. "You deserve it," Todd said warmly, giving Elizabeth a big kiss. "I'm so proud of you."

"While we're all in the same place," Mr. Collins said with a smile, taking the microphone from Mrs. Morrow, "I'd just like to announce the results of the students' centennial presidential election. The winner," he said with a big smile, "is Bruce Patman."

Once again the audience burst into applause. "Oh, Todd, I'm so happy for him," Elizabeth said warmly.

"He's right over there," Todd told her, pointing across the tent. "Why don't you tell him so yourself?"

"OK," Elizabeth said, giving Todd a quick hug. "I think I will."

"Congratulations, Bruce," Elizabeth said shyly, coming up from behind and putting her hand on his shoulder. Bruce whirled around to face her, his eyes lighting up when he saw who it was.

"I think I should say the same to you," he said quietly. "You've done a great job with all this, Liz. Regina would have loved it."

Elizabeth flushed. "I guess I didn't just mean congratulations on the election," she told him softly. "I never would have guessed I'd be saying this, but I'm proud of you, Bruce. And it's not because you won the election. I think you won something much more important."

"So do I," Bruce said solemnly, looking past Elizabeth at the Morrow family. "I just hope Regina knows how I feel," he added.

"I have a feeling," Elizabeth told him, "that she does."

"Whoever heard of having a reunion party for something that took place just two weeks ago?" Jessica grumbled to Elizabeth. It was Friday afternoon, and the twins were sitting out on the green lawn in front of Sweet Valley High.

"It was Todd's idea, and I think it's a good one," Elizabeth told her sister.

"Just because you were the star of the carnival," Jessica muttered, "you want to drag it out forever."

"Jess!" Elizabeth exclaimed indignantly. "That isn't true at all. It so happens that today's the day Mr. Collins is making the donation to the hospital. We raised over eight hundred dollars! Isn't that cause enough to celebrate?"

"I suppose so." Jessica sighed. She was scanning the lawn for someone, and Elizabeth could tell her mind wasn't really on their conversation.

"What's wrong with you today, anyway?" Elizabeth asked her. "Since when do you turn your nose up at the chance for a good party?"

"Nothing's wrong," Jessica said shortly, swatting at a mosquito with the paper she'd rolled up into a tube.

"What's that?" Elizabeth asked. "Is that your term paper?"

"Sorry, Liz," Jessica burst out unceremoniously. "I've got to go." She had just spotted Lila across the lawn, and within seconds she had sped over to confront her.

"Lila Fowler," she said angrily, "don't you feel the tiniest bit sorry about what's happened?"

"What's happened where?" Lila asked innocently, brushing a bit of nonexistent dirt from the front of her new white trousers. Lila was planning to drop by her father's building again this afternoon, and she wanted to make sure she looked her best.

"Here!" Jessica shrieked indignantly, unrolling the paper in her hand and waving it in front of Lila's eyes. "*This* is what I'm talking about!"

"Oh, dear," Lila said, looking down at the big red D marked on the top of the paper. "Jessica, please see me" was written under the grade.

"Is that all you can say?" Jessica muttered. "Did you get yours back yet?"

Lila hesitated. "Of course," she admitted finally. "We all got them back today, Jess. You know that."

"And how'd you do on it?" Jessica demanded.

"OK," Lila said noncommittally. "Come on, Jess—I'm really in a hurry. Can't we talk about this later?"

"No," Jessica fumed, "we can't. Just how good is 'OK'?"

"I got a B-minus," Lila admitted. "But I still can't see why you're making such a fuss, Jessica. I *tried* my hardest. I just—"

"If you tried your hardest and got a D on my paper, how'd you manage to get a B-minus on your own?" Jessica demanded.

Lila shrugged, her eyes wide with innocence. "I guess I was just tired," she said apologetically.

"You know how it is, Jess. I did mine first, and by the time I got around to yours—"

"That's great, Lila," Jessica snapped. "Really great. Do you realize that term paper could keep me from passing history?"

Lila shrugged. "It won't, will it?" she asked sweetly.

Jessica stared at her. "It won't, if I do OK on the final, but—"

"Good," Lila said firmly. "Then it's all right."

Jessica didn't look convinced.

"Who cares about history, anyway?" Lila said airily. "Guess where I'm going right now?" she asked, dropping her voice.

"Where?" Jessica asked. *As if I care*, she thought moodily. Jessica didn't share Lila's nonchalance about her term paper. She'd had a harrowing talk wtih Mr. Fellows about it, and now she'd have to work extra hard on the final exam or she'd fail for sure.

"I'm going over to my father's building to see if Jack is around," Lila told her. "I'm almost positive he'll ask me out this time," she added.

"Maybe he'll ask you to help him write a term paper," Jessica suggested, irritated by Lila's smugness. Jessica just wasn't in the mood for Lila. Aside from the rotten grade she'd gotten on her paper, she was depressed because she'd gotten a letter from Donald the day before, apologizing for not getting in touch with her before the carnival. He hadn't wanted to lead her on, the letter said. *Lead me on!* Jessica thought sadly. I'm all washed up. Sixteen years old and over the hill.

"Jess, I'm telling you, he's fabulous," Lila said.

Jessica stared at her, the sparkle coming back to her blue-green eyes. "Tell me more about him," she said impulsively.

Her face brightening, Lila leaned forward, launching into a lengthy description of Jack's charms.

And Jessica listened avidly. It had just occurred to her that Lila might need a dose of her own medicine. And maybe—if Jessica could get to know this Jack character herself—she just might be able to get that smirk off Lila's face for good!

Fifteen minutes later, Lila parked her car in front of her father's new building. Frantically checking her appearance in the rearview mirror, Lila bounded out of the car and strolled casually over to the fence closing in the construction site.

"Jack!" she called, waving at the group of men moving iron girders with heavy machinery. A minute later Jack separated himself from the group and sauntered over to the fence.

"Lila Fowler," he said lazily, grinning down at

her with his green-flecked eyes. "What brings you back to this territory?"

"Oh, I don't know," she said coyly, shrugging her shoulders and looking up at him with her most flirtatious smile. "I was just thinking about my plans for the summer. I wanted to talk to Daddy about going to Europe," she lied.

"Really?" Jack said, folding his arms on top of the fence and putting his chin on his arms. "Where in Europe?"

"Oh, I don't know," Lila said, thinking quickly. "Maybe the Riviera."

Jack smiled. "I used to go sailing off the south of France," he told her.

Lila's breath caught in her throat. That absolutely settled it as far as she was concerned. Whoever this Jack was, he wasn't *really* a construction worker. He was far too sophisticated, too refined.

"Do you have a boat? It's been so hot," she added softly. "I'll bet it feels just terrific out on the water."

"It sure does," Jack agreed, half-closing his eyes. "I *do* have a boat," he told her. "And I wouldn't mind being out on her right this minute," he added.

Why aren't you? Lila wanted to ask him. *What are you doing here, dragging these heavy pieces of lumber around on such a beautiful day?* But she controlled herself. First things first. Once Jack

149

had fallen in love with her, he'd reveal his real identity to her. Then maybe he'd whisk her away to the south of France and introduce her to his family. Lila was convinced by now that he was only working here as a disguise. His *real* family was probably filthy rich.

But first she had to get him to ask her out. And he didn't seem to be jumping at the bait for some reason. "They say the weather's supposed to be perfect for sailing tomorrow," Lila said, trying again.

"That's good news," Jack said, smiling that mysterious, slow smile.

Lila thought quickly. Jack didn't seem to be taking a hint, so she'd have to try the direct approach. "You know," she said suddenly, "a bunch of us have been planning a swimming party at my place on Sunday. You wouldn't want to drop by, would you?"

"Sure," Jack said. "That sounds nice."

Lila flushed. She felt strangely insecure with Jack, though she couldn't tell why. He couldn't possibly know that she had just decided to have a party right then, but something in his eyes made her feel that he was looking right through her. His smile had a slightly ironic look that made Lila's heart beat faster.

"Here," she said quickly. "Let me give you directions to my house. Can you come by around two o'clock?" she asked, taking a piece of paper from her purse and frantically writing on it.

"I'll be looking forward to it," Jack said, grinning as he took the piece of paper Lila handed him through the fence.

"Happy sailing!" Lila called after him. Jack wriggled his fingers in a backward wave, not turning around. *What a stupid thing to say*, Lila thought. *He's going to think I'm too dumb to talk about anything but boats.*

Whirling around, Lila almost bumped smack into Marcia Forbes, her father's secretary. "Marcia!" she exclaimed, trying to retain her composure.

"How are you, Lila?" Ms. Forbes asked, looking at Lila a little strangely. "Did you want to see your father?"

Lila nodded, too surprised to speak.

"He's upstairs," Ms. Forbes said. "I have to run an errand, but I'm sure you two won't need me."

Lila knew that she had no choice now; she would have to stop in at her father's office. *I wonder if she saw me talking to Jack*, Lila thought, hurrying toward the office. *Not that it would matter if she did. It won't be long now before the whole world knows!*

Lila felt as if she were floating as she opened the door to her father's office. She had no idea what excuse she could give for visiting him. All she knew was that she was falling head over heels in love and that she had to wait until Sunday before she got to see her mysterious prince again.

Will Jack destroy Lila and Jessica's friendship? Find out in Sweet Valley High #19, SHOWDOWN.

A LETTER TO THE READER

Dear Friend,

Ever since I created the series, SWEET VALLEY HIGH, I've been thinking about a love trilogy, a miniseries revolving around one very special girl, a character similar in some ways to Jessica Wakefield, but even more devastating—more beautiful, more charming, and much more devious.

Her name is Caitlin Ryan, and with her long black hair, her magnificent blue eyes and ivory complexion, she's the most popular girl at the exclusive boarding school she attends in Virginia. On the surface her life seems perfect. She has it all: great wealth, talent, intelligence, and the dazzle to charm every boy in the school. But deep inside there's a secret need that haunts her life.

Caitlin's mother died in childbirth, and her father abandoned her immediately after she was born. At least that's the lie she has been told by her enormously rich grandmother, the cold and powerful matriarch who has raised Caitlin and given her everything money can buy. But not love.

Caitlin dances from boy to boy, never staying long, often breaking hearts, yet she's so sparkling and delightful that everyone forgives her. No one can resist her.

No one that is, but Jed Michaels. He's the new boy in school—tall, wonderfully handsome, and very, very nice. And Caitlin means to have him.

But somehow the old tricks don't work; she can't

seem to manipulate him. Impossible! There has never been anyone that the beautiful and terrible Caitlin couldn't have. And now she wants Jed Michaels—no matter who gets hurt or what she has to do to get him.

So many of you follow my SWEET VALLEY HIGH series that I know you'll find it fascinating to read what happens when love comes into the life of this spoiled and selfish beauty—the indomitable Caitlin Ryan.

Thanks for being there, and keep reading,

Francine Pascal

A special preview of the exciting
opening chapter of the first book
in the fabulous new trilogy:

CAITLIN

BOOK ONE

LOVING

---

by Francine Pascal,
creator of the best-selling
SWEET VALLEY HIGH series

"That's not a bad idea, Tenny," Caitlin said as she reached for a book from her locker. "Actually, it's pretty good."

"You really like it?" Tenny Sears hung on every word the beautiful Caitlin Ryan said. It was the petite freshman's dream to be accepted into the elite group the tall, dark-haired junior led at Highgate Academy. She was ready to do anything to belong.

Caitlin looked around and noticed the group of five girls who had begun to walk their way, and she lowered her voice conspiratorially. "Let me think it over, and I'll get back to you later. Meanwhile let's just keep it between us, okay?"

"Absolutely." Tenny struggled to keep her excitement down to a whisper. The most important girl in the whole school liked her idea. "Cross my heart," she promised. "I won't breathe a word to anyone."

Tenny would have loved to continue the conversation, but at just that moment Caitlin remembered she'd left her gold pen in French class. Tenny was only too happy to race to fetch it.

The minute the younger girl was out of sight, Caitlin gathered the other girls around her.

"Hey, you guys, I just had a great idea for this year's benefit night. Want to hear it?"

Of course they wanted to hear what she had to say about the benefit, the profits of which would go to the scholarship fund for miners' children. Everyone was always interested in anything Caitlin Ryan had to say. She waited until all eyes were on her, then hesitated for an instant, increasing the dramatic impact of her words.

"How about a male beauty contest?"

"A what?" Morgan Conway exclaimed.

"A male beauty contest," Caitlin answered, completely unruffled. "With all the guys dressing up in crazy outfits. It'd be a sellout!"

Most of the girls looked at Caitlin as if she'd suddenly gone crazy, but Dorothy Raite, a sleek, blond newcomer to Highgate, stepped closer to Caitlin's locker. "I think it's a great idea!"

"Thanks, Dorothy," Caitlin said, smiling modestly.

"I don't know." Morgan was doubtful. "How are you going to get the guys to go along with this? I can't quite picture Roger Wake parading around on stage in a swimsuit."

"He'll be the first contestant to sign up when I get done talking to him." Caitlin's tone was slyly smug.

"And all the other guys?"

"They'll follow along." Caitlin placed the last of her books in her knapsack, zipped it shut, then gracefully slung it over her shoulder. "Everybody who's anybody in this school will just shrivel up and die if they can't be part of it. Believe me, I wouldn't let the student council down. After all, I've got my new presidency to live up to."

Morgan frowned. "I suppose." She took a chocolate bar out of her brown leather shoulder bag and began to unwrap it.

Just at that moment, Tenny came back, empty-handed and full of apologies. "Sorry, Caitlin, I asked all over, but nobody's seen it."

"That's okay. I think I left it in my room, anyway."

"Did you lose something?" Kim Verdi asked, but Caitlin dismissed the subject, saying it wasn't important.

For an instant Tenny was confused until Dorothy Raite asked her if she'd heard Caitlin's fabulous new idea for a male beauty contest. Then everything fell into place. Caitlin had sent her away in order to take credit for the idea.

It didn't even take three seconds for Tenny to make up her mind about what to do. "Sounds terrific," she said. Tenny Sears was determined to belong to this group, no matter what.

Dorothy leaned over and whispered to Caitlin. "Speaking of beauties, look who's walking over here."

Casually Caitlin glanced up at the approaching Highgate soccer star. Roger Wake's handsome face broke into a smile when he saw her. Caitlin knew he was interested in her, and up until then she'd offhandedly played with that interest—when she was in the mood.

"And look who's with him!" Dorothy's elbow nearly poked a hole in Caitlin's ribs. "Jed Michaels. Oh, my God, I've been absolutely dying to meet this guy."

Caitlin nodded, her eyes narrowing. She'd been anxious to meet Jed, too, but she didn't tell Dorothy that. Ever since his arrival as a transfer student at Highgate, Caitlin had been studying him, waiting for precisely the right moment to be introduced and to make an unforgettable impression on him. It seemed that the opportunity had just been handed to her.

"Hey, Caitlin. How're you doing?" Roger called out, completely ignoring the other girls in the group.

"Great, Roger. How about you?" Caitlin's smile couldn't have been wider. "Thought you'd be on the soccer field by now."

"I'm on my way. The coach pushed back practice half an hour today, anyway. Speaking of which, I don't remember seeing you at the last scrimmage." There was a hint of teasing in his voice.

Caitlin looked puzzled and touched her fingertips to her lips. "I was there, I'm sure—"

"We were late, Caitlin, remember?" Tenny spoke up eagerly. "I was with you at drama club, and it ran over."

"Now, how could I have forgotten? You see,

Roger"—Caitlin sent him a sly, laughing look—"we never let the team down. Jenny should know—she's one of your biggest fans."

"Tenny," the girl corrected meekly. But she was glowing from having been singled out for attention by Caitlin.

"Oh, right, Tenny. Sorry, but I'm really bad with names sometimes." Caitlin smiled at the girl with seeming sincerity, but her attention returned quickly to the two boys standing nearby.

"Caitlin," Dorothy burst in, "do you want to tell him—"

"Shhh," Caitlin put her finger to her lips. "Not yet. We haven't made all our plans."

"Tell me what?" Roger asked eagerly.

"Oh, just a little idea we have for the council fund-raiser, but it's too soon to talk about it."

"Come on." Roger was becoming intrigued. "You're not being fair, Caitlin."

She paused. "Well, since you're our star soccer player, I can tell you it's going to be the hottest happening at Highgate this fall."

"Oh, yeah? What, a party?"

"No."

"A concert?"

She shook her head, her black-lashed, blue eyes twinkling. "I'm not going to stand here and play Twenty Questions with you, Roger. But when we decide to make our plans public, you'll be the first to know. I promise."

"Guess I'll have to settle for that."

"Anyway, Roger, I promise not to let any of this other stuff interfere with my supporting the team from now on."

At her look, Roger seemed ready to melt into his Nikes.

Just at that moment Jed Michaels stepped forward. It was a casual move on his part, as though he were just leaning in a little more closely to hear the conversation. His gaze rested on Caitlin.

Although she'd deliberately given the impression of being impervious to Jed, Caitlin was acutely aware of every move he made. She'd studied him enough from a distance to know that she liked what she saw.

Six feet tall, with broad shoulders and a trim body used to exercise, Jed Michaels was the type of boy made for a girl like Caitlin. He had wavy, light brown hair, ruggedly even features, and an endearing, crooked smile. Dressed casually in a striped cotton shirt, tight cords, and western boots, Jed didn't look like the typical preppy Highgate student, and Caitlin had the feeling it was a deliberate choice. He looked like his own person.

Caitlin had been impressed before, but now that she saw him close at hand, she felt electrified. For that brief instant when his incredible green eyes had looked directly into hers, she'd felt a tingle go up her spine.

Suddenly realizing the need for an introduction, Roger put his hand on Jed's shoulder. "By the way, do you girls know Jed Michaels? He just transferred here from Montana. We've already got him signed up for the soccer team."

Immediately the girls called out a chorus of enthusiastic greetings, which Jed acknowledged with a friendly smile and a nod of his head. "Nice to meet you." Dorothy's call had been the loudest, and Jed's gaze went toward the pretty blonde.

Dorothy smiled at him warmly, and Jed grinned back. But before another word could be spoken, Caitlin riveted Jed with her most magnetic look.

"I've seen you in the halls, Jed, and hoped you'd been made welcome." The intense fire of her deep blue eyes emphasized her words.

He looked from Dorothy to Caitlin. "Sure have."

"And how do you like Highgate?" Caitlin pressed on quickly, keeping the attention on herself.

"So far, so good." His voice was deep and soft and just slightly tinged with a western drawl.

"I'm glad." The enticing smile never left Caitlin's lips. "What school did you transfer from?"

"A small one back in Montana. You wouldn't have heard of it."

"Way out in cattle country?"

His eyes glimmered. "You've been to Montana?"

"Once. Years ago with my grandmother. It's really beautiful. All those mountains . . ."

"Yeah. Our ranch borders the Rockies."

"Ranch, huh? I'll bet you ride, then."

"Before I could walk."

"Then you'll have to try the riding here—eastern style. It's really fantastic! We're known for our hunt country in this part of Virginia."

"I'd like to try it."

"Come out with me sometime, and I'll show you the trails. I ride almost every afternoon." Caitlin drew her fingers through her long, black hair, pulling it away from her face in a way she knew was becoming, yet which seemed terribly innocent.

"Sounds like something I'd enjoy,"—Jed said, smiling—"once I get settled in."

"We're not going to give him much time for riding," Roger interrupted. "Not until after soccer season, anyway. The coach already has him singled out as first-string forward."

"We're glad you're on the team," Caitlin said. "With Roger as captain, we're going to have a great season." Caitlin glanced at Roger, who seemed flattered by her praise. Then through slightly lowered lashes, she looked directly back at Jed. "But I know it will be even better now."

Jed only smiled. "Hope I can live up to that."

Roger turned to Jed. "We've got to go."

"Fine." Jed nodded.

Caitlin noticed Dorothy, who had been silent during Jed and Caitlin's conversation. She was now staring at Jed wistfully as he and Roger headed toward the door.

Caitlin quickly leaned over to whisper, "Dorothy, did you notice the way Roger was looking at you?"

Her attention instantly diverted, Dorothy looked away from Jed to look at Caitlin. "Me?" She sounded surprised.

"Yeah. He really seems interested."

"Oh, I don't think so." Despite her attraction to Jed, Dorothy seemed flattered. "He's hardly ever looked at me before."

"You were standing behind me and probably couldn't notice, but take my word for it."

Dorothy glanced at the star soccer player's retreating back. Her expression was doubtful, but for the moment she'd forgotten her pursuit of Jed, and Caitlin took that opportunity to focus her own attention on the new boy from Montana. She knew she only had a moment more to make that unforgettable impression on him before the two boys were gone. Quickly she walked forward. Her voice was light but loud enough to carry to the girls behind her.

"We were just going in your direction, anyway," she called. "Why don't we walk along just to show you what strong supporters of the team we are?"

Looking surprised, Roger said, "That's fine by us. Right, Jed?"

"Whatever you say."

Caitlin thought he sounded pleased by the attention. Quickly, before the other girls joined them, she stepped between the two boys. Roger immediately tried to pull her hand close to his side. She wanted to swat him off, but instead, gave his hand a squeeze, then let go. She was pleased when Diana fell in step beside Roger. Turning to Jed, Caitlin smiled and said, "There must be a thousand questions you still have about the school and the area. Have you been to Virginia before?"

"A few times. I've seen a little of the countryside."

"And you like it?"

As they walked out the door of the building, Jed turned his head so that he could look down into her upturned face and nodded. There was a bright twinkle in his eyes.

Caitlin took that twinkle as encouragement, and her own eyes grew brighter. "So much goes on around here at this time of year. Has anyone told you about the fall dance this weekend?"

"I think Matt Jenks did. I'm rooming with him."

"It'll be great—a real good band," Caitlin cooed. In the background she heard the sound of the others' voices, but they didn't matter. Jed Michaels was listening to *her*.

They walked together for only another minute, down the brick footpath that connected the classroom buildings to the rest of the elegant campus. Caitlin told him all she could about the upcoming dance, stopping short of asking him to be her date. She wasn't going to throw herself at him. She wouldn't have to, anyway. She knew it would be only a matter of time before he would be hers.

It didn't take them long to reach the turnoff for the soccer field. "I guess this is where I get off," she said lightly. "See you around."

"See you soon," he answered and left.

Caitlin smiled to herself. This handsome boy from Montana wasn't going to be an easy mark, but this was an adequate beginning. She wanted him—and what Caitlin wanted, Caitlin got.

"You going back to the dorm, Caitlin?" Morgan asked.

"Yeah, I've got a ton of reading to do for English lit." Caitlin spoke easily, but her thoughts were on the smile Jed Michaels had given her just before he'd left.

"Somerson really piled it on tonight, didn't she?" Gloria Parks muttered.

"Who cares about homework," Caitlin replied. "I want to hear what you guys think of Jed."

"Not bad at all." Tenny giggled.

"We ought to be asking *you*, Caitlin," Morgan added. "You got all his attention."

Caitlin brought her thoughts back to the present and laughed. "Did I? I hadn't even noticed," she said coyly.

"At least Roger's got some competition now," Jessica Stark, a usually quiet redhead, remarked. "He was really getting *unbearable*."

"There's probably a lot more to Roger than meets the eye," Dorothy said in his defense.

"I agree. Roger's not bad. And what do you expect," Caitlin added, "when all he hears is how he's the school star."

The girls started crossing the lawns from the grouping of Highgate classroom buildings toward the dorms. The magnificent grounds of the exclusive boarding school were spread out around them. The ivy-covered walls of the original school building had changed little in the two hundred years since it had been constructed as the manor house for a prosperous plantation. A sweeping carpet of lawn had replaced the tilled fields of the past; and the smaller buildings had been converted into dormitories and staff quarters. The horse stable had been expanded, and several structures had been added—classroom buildings, a gymnasium complete with an indoor pool, tennis and racketball courts—but the architecture of the new buildings blended in well with that of the old.

"Caitlin, isn't that your grandmother's car in the visitors' parking lot?" Morgan pointed toward the graveled parking area off the oak-shaded main drive. A sleek, silver Mercedes sports coupe was gleaming in the sunlight there.

"So it is." Caitlin frowned momentarily. "Wonder what she's doing here? I must have left something at the house last time I was home for the weekend."

"My dream car!" Gloria exclaimed, holding one hand up to adjust her glasses. "I've told Daddy he absolutely *must* buy me one for my sixteenth birthday."

"And what did he say?" Jessica asked.

Gloria made a face. "That I had to settle for his three-year-old Datsun or get a bicycle."

"Beats walking," Morgan said, reaching into her bag for another candy bar.

"But I'm dying to have a car like your grandmother's."

"It's not bad." Caitlin glanced up at the car. "She has the Bentley, too, but this is the car she uses when she wants to drive herself instead of being chauffeured."

"Think she'll let you bring it here for your senior year?"

Caitlin shrugged and mimicked her grandmother's cultured tones. "'It's not wise to spoil one.' Besides, I've always preferred Jaguars."

Caitlin paused on the brick path, and the other girls stopped beside her. "You know, I really should go say hello to my grandmother. She's probably waiting for me." She turned quickly to the others. "We've got to have a meeting for this fundraiser. How about tonight—my room, at seven?"

"Sure."

"Great."

"Darn, I've got to study for an exam tomorrow," Jessica grumbled, "but let me know what you decide."

"Me, too," Kim commented. "I was on the courts all afternoon yesterday practicing for Sunday's tennis tournament and really got behind with my studying."

"Okay, we'll fill you guys in, but make sure you come to the next meeting. And I don't want any excuses. If you miss the meeting, you're out!" Caitlin stressed firmly. "I'll catch the rest of you later, then."

All the girls walked away except Dorothy, who lingered behind. Just then, a tall, elegantly dressed, silver-haired woman walked briskly down the stairs from the administrative office in the main school building. She moved directly toward the Mercedes, quickly opened the driver's door, and slid in behind the wheel.

Caitlin's arm shot up in greeting, but Regina Ryan

never glanced her way. Instead, she started the engine and immediately swung out of the parking area and down the curving drive.

For an instant Caitlin stopped in her tracks. Then with a wide, carefree smile, she turned back to Dorothy and laughed. "I just remembered. She called last night and said she was dropping off my allowance money but would be in a hurry and couldn't stay. My memory really *is* bad. I'll run over and pick it up now."

As Caitlin turned, Dorothy lightly grabbed Caitlin's elbow and spoke softly. "I know you're in a hurry, but can I talk to you for a second, Caitlin? Did you mean what you said about Roger? Was he really looking at me?"

"I told you he was," Caitlin said impatiently, anxious to get Dorothy out of the picture. "Would I lie to you?"

"Oh, no. It's just that when I went over to talk to him, he didn't seem that interested. He was more interested in listening to what you and Jed were saying."

"Roger's just nosy."

"Well, I wondered. You know, I haven't had any dates since I transferred—"

"Dorothy! You're worried about dates? Are you crazy?" Caitlin grinned broadly. "And as far as Roger goes, wait and see. Believe me." She gave a breezy wave. "I've got to go."

"Yeah, okay. And, thanks, Caitlin."

"Anytime."

Without a backward glance, Caitlin walked quickly to the administration office. The story about her allowance had been a fabrication. Regina Ryan had given Caitlin more than enough spending money when she'd been home two weeks earlier, but it would be all over campus in a minute if the girls thought there was anything marring Caitlin's seemingly perfect life.

Running up the steps and across the main marble-floored lobby that had once been the elegant entrance hall of the plantation house, she walked quickly into the dean's office and smiled warmly at Mrs. Forbes, the dean's secretary.

"Hi, Mrs. Forbes."

"Hello, Caitlin. Can I help you?"

"I came to pick up the message my grandmother just left."

"Message?" Mrs. Forbes frowned.

"Yes." Caitlin continued to look cheerful. "I just saw her leaving and figured she was in a hurry and left a message for me here."

"No, she just met on some school board business briefly with Dean Fleming."

"She didn't leave anything for me?"

"I can check with the part-time girl if you like."

"Thanks." Caitlin's smile had faded, but she waited as Mrs. Forbes stepped into a small room at the rear.

She returned in a second, shaking her head. "Sorry, Caitlin."

Caitlin forced herself to smile. "No problem, Mrs. Forbes. It wasn't important, anyway. She'll probably be on the phone with me ten times tonight."

As Caitlin hurried from the main building and set out again toward the dorm, her beautiful face was grim. Why was she always trying to fool herself? She knew there was no chance her grandmother would call just to say hello. But nobody would ever know that: She would make certain of it. Not Mrs. Forbes, or any of the kids; not even her roommate, Ginny. Not anyone!

Like it so far? Want to read more? LOVING will be available in May 1985.* It will be on sale wherever Bantam paperbacks are sold. The other two books in the trilogy, LOVE DENIED and TRUE LOVE, will also be published in 1985.

*Outside the United States and Canada, books will be available approximately three months later. Check with your local bookseller for further details.

SWEET VALLEY HIGH

Prices and availability subject to change without notice.

Buy them at your local bookstore or use this convenient coupon for ordering:

BANTAM SHOP·AT·HOME C·A·T·A·L·O·G

Special Offer
Buy a Bantam Book
for only 50¢.

Now you can order the exciting books you've been wanting to read straight from Bantam's latest catalog of hundreds of titles. *And* this special offer gives you the opportunity to purchase a Bantam book for only 50¢. Here's how:

By ordering any five books at the regular price per order, you can also choose any other single book listed (up to a $5.95 value) for only 50¢. Some restrictions do apply, so for further details send for Bantam's catalog of titles today.

Just send us your name and address and we'll send you Bantam Book's SHOP AT HOME CATALOG!